CAPACITY FOR DESIRE

A Novel by

L.J. Bowen

Copyright 2019 © L.J. Bowen

Published by Major Key Publishing

www.majorkeypublishing.com

ALL RIGHTS RESERVED.

Any unauthorized reprint or use of the material is prohibited. No part of this book may be reproduced or transmitted in any form or by any means, electronic, or mechanical, including photocopying, recording, or by any information storage without express permission by the publisher.

This is an original work of fiction. Names, characters, places and incidents are either products of the author's imagination or are used fictitiously and any resemblance to actual persons, living or dead is entirely coincidental.

Contains explicit language & adult themes suitable for ages 16+

To submit a manuscript for our review, email us at
submissions@majorkeypublishing.com

Chapter 1

Brie Calhoun looked around the banquet hall and nodded with approval. The final touch had been added to her father's retirement party, and everything was looking good. The room was decorated in gold and white colors that included matching balloons, table cloths, and streamers. Theodore Calhoun was retiring after thirty-five years from the hotel industry, and he was going out with a bang.

After his get-together, he and his lady friend, Tillie, were going on a cruise that would literally take them all over the world with stops in Hawaii, Mexico, Rome, and Australia. Brie was glad that he would finally be able to sit back and relax without having to worry about the goings-on at Dynasty Towers.

The thirty-floor hotel was one of the most popular and well-known hotels in Chicago. It was located off Roosevelt and Michigan Avenue and sat a few blocks from the lake and museums. It had state-of-the-art amenities that included a spa, gym, indoor and outdoor pools, and shuttle vans. Warner's, which was a five-star restaurant, was connected to it that had complimentary breakfast hours for the guests on the weekends.

There was a business center that was open 24/7 that held five computers, a small copier, and a fax machine. The hotel also housed three big banquet rooms that were often used for wedding receptions, proms, conventions, and meetings. Whenever visiting sports teams came into town to play the home teams, they made Dynasty Towers their preferred hotel, which helped boost business.

Elmo Cobb, the hotel's executive assistant manager, stood next to Brie in the Jacaranda room and nodded with a smile. He was fifteen years older than Brie and knew that Theo's daughter would take over being CEO of the hotel, but he didn't mind. This was her legacy, and he knew she was the right person to be in charge. He had a great salary, and it was a good company to work for.

"Everything looks good, Brie," Elmo said, and she grinned.

"Thank you. Is Ms. Angel coming to the party tonight?" Angel was Elmo's wife of thirty-two years, and Brie had called her Ms. Angel for as long as she could remember.

"Yes, she'll be here. It promises to be a good time

tonight," Elmo responded, and she silently agreed.

Instead of having Warner's cater the affair and dealing with their dinner crowd, Brie had hired a catering company, and she made sure to include some of her father's favorite foods like catfish, cornbread, and greens. Some of the employees, Theo's friends, and a few shareholders would be in attendance, and she knew it would be a big crowd. Brie looked at her watch and saw that it was getting close for the revelry to begin.

"I better go up and change. The caterers will be here in about an hour to start setting up." She informed him, and he nodded as she left the room. The other banquet areas had been named the Lotus and Alpinia rooms. Those three flowers had been her mother's favorites, which prompted Theo to name them as he had.

As Brie walked across the gray, tile floor of the main lobby, she greeted the employees and guests that strolled by. Wearing blue jean shorts and a White Sox shirt, Brie usually didn't dress casually, but she dressed down to help decorate for the party. She stopped at the front desk to speak to the daytime desk supervisor, Kate.

"Hi, Miss. Calhoun."

"Hello, Kate. Anything going on I should know about?"

"No. The wedding reception that's scheduled for the Lotus room just arrived to set up."

"OK, the other wedding group should arrive sometime today for the other banquet hall. Did maintenance repair the broken television in room 1313?"

"Yes, ma'am. It appeared to be the guest's fault. Apparently, some words were exchanged, and a cell phone was thrown against it. I gave the room info sheet and credit card information to Darla."

"Well, they're going to get a call from me later. I'm heading up to get dressed for the party. I have my phone, so call me if you need anything and make sure everyone working behind the desk stops by the party to get some food and cake."

Kate nodded, and Brie headed toward the elevators. She caught an empty one and rode it up to the third floor where her office was located. It also housed storage units at the end of the hall, away from the office. The second floor contained the lockers, breakroom and daycare that had a secured entrance. There were also two spare rooms on that floor in case the employees were too tired to go home after their shift or needed a place to sleep.

"Hi, Ms. Darla."

"Hey, Brie. Everything good downstairs?" Darla was an older, white receptionist who worked for her father and was happy to stay on and work for Brie part time. She was a short woman with long, black hair, a lengthy nose, and always wore a smile on her face.

"Yes. No emergencies?"

"Nope. Things are fine here."

"Good. You can actually take off if you want to," Brie said, grabbing some papers from her mailbox.

"Great, thanks. That'll give me time to go home and change for the party."

She went into her office and shut the door. It was a decent-sized room with plush, beige carpet, two mushroom-colored chairs sat in front of the wide, oak desk that was big enough to hold a desktop and a printer sat in the corner. Three tall windows were behind the desk that had vertical blinds and faced the lake. There was a small, red sofa to the right of the desk with several throw pillows and a small restroom was a few feet from the couch.

Brie sat down on the black, leather chair and leaned back to relax. She was an average-height woman with light-brown skin and dark-brown hair that rested at her shoulders. Her eyebrows were naturally arched, and she had coffee-colored, almond-shaped eyes that fit well with her small nose and full lips.

She had been CEO in training for two years and was ready to handle things by herself. Sometimes she still got amazed that a small bed-and-breakfast had turned into this huge empire. It had been her parent's dream to have a prosperous B&B that would expand across the world. However, when Brie's mother passed from cancer at the age of forty-seven, Theo kept his promise to his wife to look after their daughter and to pursue their dream.

Even though she was young when her mother died, Brie still missed her, and she knew Cassie Calhoun would be proud of what her family had accomplished. Brie also knew her mother wouldn't want Theo to mourn forever, and somehow felt Cassie approved of Tillie, who looked like she could be Tina Turner's cousin.

As she got up to head toward the private bath, the elevator doors opened, and she could hear her best friend, Qyle, talking on the phone and heading for the office. Qyle had a big, loud voice that carried and had a slight accent. Brie turned on the shower just as she was finishing the conversation.

"Hey, my client doesn't want to do some stereotypical commercial. Either the idea concept is changed or we walk. Believe me, the people at Mystic Drinks would be glad for my phone call." Qyle waved at her friend as she undid the jacket of her cinnamon-colored pantsuit, and Brie closed the door to the bathroom.

"Good. Idea number two is better and more family oriented. We'll be there tomorrow night. Have a good day." She flipped the Nokia cell phone closed after texting her client the details of the call.

Qyle Montoya was a hell of a sports agent, and she went all in for her clients. She represented eleven athletes: four football, five basketball, and two baseball players. She had been on the phone about the rookie baseball player, Ernesto Galvan, who had just signed a four-year, six-figure contract and was trying to seal the deal for him to be the new spokesperson for an energy sports drink.

Most sports players would be nervous or apprehensive about having a female agent, but Qyle's reputation easily rivaled her male counterparts. She was three feet taller than Brie, had a husky frame, and she wore her sleek, black hair in a buzz cut. The two had met at a professional women's expo five years ago and had been friends since.

"I'll be out in a minute, Qyle."

"Take your time." She looked out the window and liked the cool breeze that flowed in from the open windows. It was a nice May afternoon, and she could see people taking advantage of the good weather by being outdoors and enjoying their time at the beach. Tourists and residents who strolled at a relaxed pace could also be seen from the windows and they weren't in a hurry to get to their destinations. Minutes after the shower turned off, Brie opened the door, and Qyle looked at her.

She knew Brie wasn't gay and appreciated their relationship, but that didn't stop Qyle from having more than friendship love for Brie. Of course, the latter didn't know about Qyle's feelings, and she would never find out.

"Who were you yelling at?" Brie had slipped on a pale-pink cocktail dress with matching high heels and her mother's pearl necklace and earrings.

"The director from Extreme Striker drinks. He wanted to put Ernesto in some stereotypical East LA bullshit type commercial, and I told him to change the concept or he's walking."

"So what happened?"

"He switched it to the family-style one. It should air in a few months after they shoot it."

"Good job, Qyle." Brie had finished applying her Bath and Body Works lotion and looked at her best friend. "Thanks for coming to the party," Brie mentioned, and Qyle waved the words away.

"No worries. I can sit back and kick it tonight. I'm glad Papa Theo is retiring and getting away for a while. I know you're going to miss him," Qyle said genuinely.

Brie internally acknowledged her friend's words. It had been just the two of them for years. Theo had done his best to not smother Brie, and she tried not to be overprotective of him.

"I will miss him, but he'll be fine on the cruise. He has

Tillie to keep him company."

"And how long will they be gone?" Qyle asked, arranging the pearls around Brie's neck.

"At least four months, I believe."

"Has Faith gotten here yet?"

"I spoke to her a few hours ago. She's going to come here straight from the airport and stay with me for the night. She has an early flight back to LA in the morning."

It had been a while since the three of them had gotten together and Qyle was looking forward to hanging out with her girls.

"We should head downstairs. I need to check to see if the DJ has shown up yet."

The two women went back downstairs, and Brie was glad that the DJ had arrived and was playing The O'Jays. Brie had wanted it to be a surprise party, but the cat was let out the bag when Theo accidently overheard Elmo talking about the party to some employees. He promised he'd act surprised, and Brie told him he didn't have to.

The banquet hall was an oblong-shaped room with a shiny wooden floor that had a metal barrier to separate the dance section of the flooring. There were square tables that could seat eight people, and it was decorated in a white table cloth and the centerpieces were paper weights that had three solid and frosted balloons to go with the color theme. Twinkling lights hung from the ceiling, and there was a stocked bar with liquor and soft drink options. On the left side was a banner that read 'Happy Retirement, Theo', and the food was set up on the right side of the room.

Seeing that the food had been set up and it was being kept warm, people on the guest list had started to arrive. At 7:30 p.m., the man of the hour showed up, looking dapper in a white linen suit. Brie was so happy that the party turned out to be a success. People were loving the soul food and free drinks that the bar supplied. She was also glad to see the hotel employee's pop in and out to congratulate Theo and get something to eat and was happy that her other best friend, Faith, had shown up to complete the evening.

Faith Daye was the third person of their group and an award-winning actress. She had starred in movies with big-time actors and had several movies on her résumé. After she won an Oscar last year, her acting career had gone through the roof. She had been asked to star in several TV shows and was currently filming a comedy with comedian Quinn Darrow but had flown to Chicago for the party. Faith was a six-foot-tall, latte-colored beauty who was always making headlines from her fashion choices to her charity works.

Faith had shown up around eight, and the friends sat down at the last empty table in the back to catch up. Faith and Brie had been friends in college, and the former had met Qyle through Brie. Faith had on a stunning, lime-colored gown, but she didn't walk around like she was better than anyone there. She had a big, buff guy as her security guard and kept waving him back when people asked for her autograph or for a picture with her.

Theo had just finished slow dancing with Tillie, and he found his daughter sipping on ice water at the bar. He gave her a long, tight hug, and she returned the sentiment.

"How do you like your party, Daddy?"

"I love it, honey. You went all out. Thank you."

"You're welcome. You deserve a big send off." Theo was a tall, dark man who still had a head full of hair that was cut low, dark-brown eyes, and a trimmed, graying goatee. He was

17

a very handsome man, and Brie was proud to be his daughter.

"Let's go talk before they bring out my cake," Theo said, and she took his arm.

"How do you know you have one?"

"I know you went to a bakery and had one of those fancy cakes made for tonight. People talk around here."

"People talk, or you listen too much?" Theo chuckled, and they went to sit on one of the loungers in front of the window. It was near the tall, glass waterfall, and Brie knew this was his favorite spot in the lobby.

Brie didn't say anything as he stared at the flowing water, knowing she had nothing to fear about what he had to say.

"I'm glad to be going, but nervous about leaving it all for you to run by yourself," Theo stated, and Brie gasped.

"You don't trust me, Daddy?"

"I'm not saying that, honey. That didn't even cross my mind. The nerves are on my part. I know you have to do things your way. I'm just being a stubborn, old man and not ready to give up the day-to-day operations."

Brie relaxed at Theo's words. He was having a hard time letting go, and she understood. The small B&B that had grown into this grand business had been his life, just like his daughter had been.

She leaned over and took his hand. "If you feel that way, you can stay, and I can take your place on that fantastic cruise," she replied with a knowing grin.

"Hell no! Tillie and I are looking forward to it, and we need to unwind." Tillie had retired a few months ago from being an accountant, and the cruise was all she talked about. Her husband had passed away some years ago, and her only son lived in Cleveland. Brie liked the fact that they were two nice people who had found love again and were enjoying their time together.

"Daddy, I know how you feel about the hotel. I have your business sense, and I'm a Calhoun. You can enjoy your vacation knowing Dynasty Towers is in good hands with me."

"I'm not worried that you're going to run the place into the ground, Brie. But you are young and should be dating or a least have a boyfriend. I don't want you to not have a personal life on account of the hotel," Theo explained, and she let out a small breath.

It's true that she didn't date much, and she was still young, but she had a job to do and a huge responsibility on her shoulders now. It would be plenty of time for that other stuff later.

"Daddy, I'm only thirty years old, and I'm not worried about that right now. I love being involved with everything that is going on. I know that's how you did it, and everything was in order because of your management style. Do you think the employees would respect me or care about their jobs if I was out partying every night and neglecting things here?"

Theo released a deep breath and looked at his daughter. She looked so much like Cassie it almost bought a tear to his eye. "I know, but don't let being CEO consume you."

She leaned over and gave him a soft peck on his cheek. "You're such a Daddy."

"I know. Is everything all set for the meeting with S&T Construction next week?"

"I'm on top of it. The meeting was confirmed, and I have the blueprints to take with me."

"I sure wish this deal had been finalized before I left for our trip."

"Honestly, I'm glad it didn't. I like being the one to start and finish out negotiations for the lot next door. When you get back, the renovations should be started, and that can put your mind at ease."

Theo squeezed her hand and grinned. "I know, honey. I also know the hotel will prosper with you at the helm. I trust you completely, and you don't have to call me for any advice on anything." He stood up at that and helped Brie to stand as well.

"I wasn't going to call you," she retorted with a natural smile, laughing at his facial expression. They went back into the room just as the extravagant, three-tier lemon cake was brought out, and the gathering continued for the next few hours with laughter and fun.

****

Marshall Thornton knocked on Xander Sterling's office door and opened it when he got permission to enter. His best friend and former teammate was typing something on the computer, and Marshall waited until he was done before speaking. S&T Construction offices were located on 18th Street in the South Loop area away from the crowds and traffic congestion of the downtown area.

Marshall was half owner of the company with Xander, and it was a profitable one. It was a successful business that had won the bid to build several buildings in the city that included the new recreational center next to the United Center and the new radiology department to the Riverside Hospital.

S&T got started years ago, and of course it took some time for the establishment to get off the ground. But once a few small jobs let to bigger ones, they had expanded their operations and was able to hire more workers. Because of the work they had done, S&T started obtaining jobs outside the city, and that was good news for everyone involved. It allowed the construction workers to continue to work and provide for themselves and families, and it put the business on the map as a competitive heavy hitter.

The two men had known each other since their last year of college and were fraternity brothers. Marshall was wearing a navy suit with a red tie, and Xander was sporting black trousers with a maroon button-down shirt. The latter was a tall black man who had a skin-fade haircut. He had a soft-chocolate complexion and striking, light-brown eyes.

"Hey, man. What's up?"

"Miss Calhoun will be here in a few minutes. You ready for the meeting?" Marshall asked, and Xander nodded.

"Yes, I'm just finishing up an email."

"This is a big deal for the company, contracting with Dynasty Towers," Marshall stated, and Xander chuckled softly.

"You always say a bid is a big deal for the company, but I agree. I'm glad Mr. Calhoun thought of us to do the add-on."

"He must've been happy with the work we previously did."

Xander stood up and put on his suit jacket before following Marshall to the conference room. It was an oval-shaped space with a big, glass table with six tan, leather cushioned chairs. The table could accommodate twelve people, but they didn't need all the chairs for the meeting. A fresh pot of coffee had been made for the client just in case, and both men had their pens and ledgers with them.

"Since Doug couldn't get away from the Plainfield job today for the meeting, he's going to make sure he's available for the walkthrough whenever it's scheduled," Marshall said to Xander, who nodded again. Doug Greenway was their foreman, who was the first person they signed under S&T, and he was a knowledgeable guy.

The phone intercom on the table buzzed, and the receptionist, Zora, spoke softly from her end, "Mr. Sterling, Mr. Thornton, Miss Calhoun is here for your noon appointment."

"Great. Please escort her to the conference room."

The guys stood up as Brie was shown to the room, and Xander's eyes widened when he saw who walked in.

"Brie?"

"Hello, Xander," she greeted with a genuine smile.

Chapter 2

"You two know each other?" Marshall asked with surprise, and the two people didn't immediately answer the question.

Xander didn't think in a million years Brie Calhoun would've walked into the room looking... well, hell, looking good. He hadn't laid eyes on her since their junior year of college and didn't think he would've seen her again.

"Miss Calhoun, I'm Marshall Thornton. I believe somehow you already know my business associate, Xander Sterling." Marshall introduced himself when they didn't say anything, and they shook hands.

"It's nice to meet you. To answer your question, yes. We went to college together."

"You went to U of I too? I don't remember meeting you, but I digress. Please have a seat. Would you like something to drink?"

"No, thank you." The trio sat down; the shock finally wearing off with Xander.

"You're Theodore Calhoun's daughter?" Xander asked, and she looked at him from across the table.

"Yes. I've just taken over as CEO of the hotel. My father is officially retired." She informed them, and both men looked startled.

"Oh, that's surprising," Marshall said.

"Why do you say that, Mr. Thornton?"

"I meant no disrespect. It's just that your dad was always so hands- on with the hotel. It's hard to picture him retiring from it all," he explained, and she chuckled.

"Oh, I agree. But he's entrusted things to me, and I'm going to maintain his legacy. His last act of CEO was to purchase the empty lot next to us to expand the hotel. It was such an eyesore, and he worked endlessly to acquire it. The papers were signed a few weeks ago, and he had such good things to say about this company and wanted to make sure I commissioned S&T to get the job done," Brie said, keeping eye contact with them with a stern voice.

Xander and Marshall could tell she had a good business awareness, and they were glad she had a level head on her shoulders.

"We certainly appreciate that. Your dad is an honest and fair man."

"Thank you. I'll be sure to tell him."

"What plans are you considering for the expansion?" Marshall asked her.

"Of course, more rooms. Two more banquet halls, another business center and spa. I'm considering presidential suites for our celebrity guests."

"Do you get a lot of celebrities?" Xander asked, making notes in his notebook.

"Visiting sports teams frequently check into Dynasty Towers, and they always request floors with no public access. I can understand the appeal because I don't want them to feel hounded or their privacy interrupted. Oh, and Faith always gets a suite of rooms when she's in town filming a movie."

"I'm sorry… Faith?"

"Faith Daye, the actress."

"She stays at the hotel?" Xander inquired with a stunned expression.

"All the time. She's one of my best friends."

"You're best friends with an award-winning actress?"

"You're starting to sound like a parrot," Marshall mumbled, and Brie flashed a half smile just as her phone rang.

"Excuse me. I need to take this."

Marshall glanced at Xander, who was seemingly impressed by Brie. He definitely had some questions about their acquaintance but could wait until the meeting was over to ask Xander.

"Hey, Elmo. What's up?"

"There's a situation with the two weddings here. The time for the pictures got double booked for the waterfall, and they're arguing about who should take them first."

"Look at the registry and see who booked their wedding first. They will be the ones who can take them at the waterfall. Show the second couple the flower garden with the arch to see if that location will suffice. To appease both couples, give them a free bottle of champagne and a free night in one of the suites for any open date this year. Call back if there are any more issues." Brie hung up her Blackberry and looked at the two men. "Sorry about that."

"It's fine. Everything OK?"

She nodded, placing the blueprints of the lot and hotel on the table. "I brought these; I don't know if you needed to look at them."

Brie watched as they stood up and carefully examined the plans. She took this time to silently observe Xander. She was beyond shocked to see him. If she had bet the hotel she'd never see Xander again in life, she would've clearly lost. It never dawned on her that Xander Sterling was the S in S&T Construction.

Because her dad had recommended them and praised their work, she didn't think to look up and research the company beforehand. She took notice of his physique. Xander was tall with broad shoulders and a narrow torso. The years had been good to him and added to his handsomeness. Her eyes skimmed along his perfectly-lined and trimmed hair, serious, yet warm eyes, smooth gingerbread-colored skin, and nice lips. He still had that small indentation in his chin that she always liked, and Brie was glad that he was doing well for himself. She also noticed a gold wedding band on his left hand.

He probably has a wife who dotes on him and a house full of kids, she said to herself.

Xander glanced up and saw Brie looking at him, and she

29

averted her eyes.

"Do you have keys to the empty building, Ms. Calhoun?" Marshall wondered, making Brie glad for the distraction.

"Yes, but I didn't bring them with me," she answered.

"That's fine. We're going to look up the building's history to see if there were any violations or structural problems. Can we meet tomorrow morning with our foreman to do a walk-through?" Marshall asked her.

"Sure. What time?"

"9:30 a.m. should be fine." Brie nodded, picking up her phone to put the reminder in her calendar.

"Make sure to wear boots in case there is broken glass or nails sticking up and about," Xander warned her.

"What will the walk-through do?" Brie questioned out of curiosity.

"It allows us to get a feel for the foundation and composition," Xander replied, and she nodded.

"Do you have any plans for landscaping?"

"I wanted to add another fountain outside. I'll have more concrete ideas by tomorrow."

"Can we hold onto these blueprints?"

"Yes, of course." They talked for another half hour before the meeting ended.

"Thank you for coming, Ms. Calhoun," Marshall said, shaking her hand again.

"Thank you both for meeting with me. I'll see you in the morning."

"Yes, we'll meet you in the hotel lobby." Brie agreed, and Marshall excused himself saying he was going to meet his wife for lunch.

Brie and Xander were left alone, eyeballing one another. She took a deep breath and decided to break the ice. "You look good, Xander."

"You too, Brie. It's good to see you."

"So I see your dreams have become a success," she mentioned, and he shrugged.

"It's just my plan-B after football."

"You're the rare few who have an efficacious life after going pro."

"Thank you, Brie. Also, congratulations on becoming CEO of the hotel." Brie lifted one shoulder, playing with the strap of her purse.

"I knew I'd take over some day. I'm just glad to be in the driver's seat." She cleared her throat as they continued to look at each other.

"Well, I better go. It was nice to see you again." She reached for the buttons for the elevator, but his words stopped her.

"Brie, if you don't have any plans right now, let's go out to lunch and catch up." She pursed her lips and glanced toward the empty conference room.

"I don't know, Xander. I don't want to keep you away from your work."

"It can wait. Have you had lunch yet?"

"No, but—"

"C'mon, it's two college friends catching up." He persisted, and a small part inside Brie was screaming that she should refuse.

"Sure. Where do you want to go?"

"I'll meet you at Del Prado's. I just have to finish some things up in my office really quick."

She nodded and headed toward the restroom. Xander entered his office, closed the door and sat at his desk, still in disbelief he had seen Brie Calhoun today. Hell, it had been years since he'd seen her, and he could remember it like it was yesterday…

Chapter 3

Twelve years ago...

Circa 1983:

Xander looked at the D on his math quiz, and his heart sank. This was the third test of the semester, and he hadn't passed one yet. He had done okay in college algebra by passing with a C, but this junior-level trigonometry class was kicking his ass, and it was one he needed to do well in for his major in business management.

He was the star quarterback on the football team at the University of Illinois Urbana-Champaign, and there was a game on Friday night. Xander was passing all his other classes with ease, but this damn class was messing up his average. Scouts had been sniffing around him, and talks of being drafted into the NFL had been whispered.

Of course, he had gotten excited about that, and he was ready to drop school to play in the big leagues. But his parents, especially his father Xen, had put his foot down about his son graduating with a degree first. Xander could hear his father sternly tell him that the NFL wasn't going anywhere, and he needed something to fall back on in case football didn't pan out.

"Xander, can I see you for a moment?" Professor Love summoned as he dismissed the class, and Xander nodded as he gathered his things.

He took his time walking down the steps of the lecture hall. He knew whatever Professor Love had to say wouldn't be good.

"Yes, sir?"

"What happened with your test, son?" Professor Love was an older, black man with a head full of white hair and a white beard. He might've looked elderly, but he was sharp as a knife.

"I don't know.. I really did study and tried my best," Xander replied, and the teacher cocked his head.

"Did you honestly put 100 percent effort into it?"

"Well… not the whole hundred, sir." The professor nodded and started to pack up his satchel.

"I see that you're trying here. You don't have all your cards stacked into having a football career, and that's why I've assigned you a tutor to help with this class," he announced, and Xander balked at that.

"Professor, thanks for that, but with everything going on,

35

I don't have time to—"

"Make the time, Xander. You're a junior now and can't afford to fail any of your classes. I've already spoken to Coach Ventura about it, and he agrees. You'll see your tutor every Tuesday and Thursday evening for the remainder of the semester. That doesn't interfere with practice, so it'll be fine," Professor Love reassured Xander, handing him a piece of paper.

He saw the information containing the location, time, and tutor's name on it and sighed.

"Professor, I—"

"This isn't up for discussion, son. Either you get help passing my class or you fail and get kicked off the team."

"What!"

"It was the coach's terms. We see a lot of potential in you, and we don't let our students fall through the cracks here at U of I. Don't feel like I'm singling you out either. You're my ninth student to get tutoring assistance," the teacher stated as he left the classroom.

Xander grunted and left a few seconds later to head towards Coach Ventura's office. *Maybe getting some help won't be too bad*, he thought.

****

Coach Caesar Ventura was looking over his playbook when Xander knocked on his office door. He was a portly white man with a full beard and slicked-back brown hair; his lucky whistle hanging around his neck.

"Hey, coach."

"Sterling, what's up?" He closed the book and sat back in his chair. His office was clean but cluttered with football memorabilia from signed balls to trading cards.

"I just left Professor Love's class."

"We're just trying to help you pass the class," he countered matter-of-factly.

"I know, and he also told me the conditions of which I have to accept the tutoring."

"Playing for U of I is a privilege, but you have to earn it and do right by your classes. I tell that to everyone who's on that field wearing the school colors." Xander knew he didn't play favoritism and wanted the team to succeed on and off the field.

Xander deeply exhaled and sat forward in the chair. He

was sporting a high-top fade, acid-washed blue jeans, and a long-sleeve blue jean button-down shirt.

"It's just your pride stinging about the tutoring suggestion. Shall I call your dad and see what he has to say?" Xander sat up at that, raising his hands.

"No, don't do that! I'm going, coach." Luckily, it was a Wednesday afternoon, and the sun was shining on a pleasant September day. He could fret about it for another day before sucking it up and taking it like a man.

"Good. Now go change for practice."

Xander nodded and left the office. Coach Ventura knew Xander's chances of going to the NFL was high, but he also knew that Xander wanted other options in case the NFL didn't work out. That was fine by the coach as he knew football wasn't a lifelong career.

Xander was unique in the game because he was ambidextrous, so he made a valuable contribution to the team. That was one of the reasons why Coach Ventura wanted Xander to play for the team. He also knew he needed to fulfill his promise to Xander's dad that his son would leave U of I with a degree. Make no mistake, he cared about all his players equally. Some were depending on a football career as their livelihood, and the others, like Xander, were looking at the bigger picture. Coach Ventura got up, grabbed the playbook, and left the office to head toward the football field.

****

Brie sat in one of the private study rooms of the school library, finishing her English paper to be typed later and exchanged the materials for her math things. She looked at her neon-pink watch and saw it was ten minutes until the hour, and Xander should be walking in any minute.

She was one of those few female students who admired Xander's sexiness and masculinity from afar. They were in the same strategic management class, but she knew he didn't know that. He was easy on the eyes, and he seemed like he was a good guy. She knew he was intelligent and a good athlete to boot.

She was taking the same lecture Professor Love was teaching to Xander's class, just on a different day. Brie had been told by Professor Love that she was one of his top students and didn't mind when he asked her to tutor Xander. Because she didn't have any starry-eyed feelings toward him, she knew their weekly meetings wouldn't cause any problems. There was a soft knock on the door, and she looked up to see him step in.

"Excuse me, are you Brie Calhoun?"

"Yes. Hi, Xander. Come in."

"You know me?" He wondered, sliding the bookbag off his shoulder and sitting in the chair across from her.

"We're in Dr. Nichols's strategic class together. I usually sit in the third row," she told him, and he looked at her with surprise.

"Really?" She nodded, and he racked his brain trying to place her in the class, but seeing how it had twenty-five students, it was difficult.

"Oh, I wasn't aware we were in the same class."

"I figured. So what's going on with your math class?"

Xander took a moment to study her. She was a cute little thing and felt bad he hadn't noticed her as his classmate. She wasn't as glamorous looking as his girlfriend, Starr, but she seemed nice enough.

"Can we talk first? Get to know one another before we jump right into it since we're going to be hanging out for a few months," he said instead, and she looked at him, playing with her pencil.

"What would you like to know?" she asked him.

"Well, what year are you? What's your major? Where are you from?"

"I'm a junior, a business major with a minor in math, and I'm from Chicago. I work behind the scenes with the drama club. Your turn," she responded, and he chuckled. He liked the dimples in her cheek when she talked.

"I'm a junior as well and a business management major. I'm the starting quarterback, and I live in the Alpha frat house."

"A frat boy, huh?" He smirked at her, and she returned it.

"Speaking of football, you should throw more with your left hand. When you throw with the right, it always curves out, and the other team can see it and intercept," Brie advised, and his eyebrows shot up.

"What?"

"You heard me."

"I did. It's just... wow. I wasn't expecting that keen observation."

"Why? Because I'm a girl?" She shot the question back at him, and he grinned.

"Honestly, yeah. It sounds like you're onto something here."

Brie shrugged at that as she shifted in the chair. "I used to watch a lot of football games with my dad when I was younger, and we would talk about it. He explained the different positions, plays, and how the ball was thrown."

"I'll keep that in mind. You're the first woman to comment on football like you know what you're talking about. Thank you for that." Her comments reminded Xander that one shouldn't judge a book by its cover.

Brie shrugged. "It's just a suggestion." Xander's eyes ran over Brie's face, and he was, again, impressed by what she said.

"So now that we've gotten past the pleasantries, what's going on with you and math?" He sighed and released his breath through puffed out cheeks.

"I suck at it, basically." She smiled softly at his words.

"There's no such thing. You just have to find a rhythm to understanding it."

"I think it's more than that," he mumbled, but she heard him.

"We're studying the same chapters in Professor Love's class, so why don't we start there?" Brie watched as he pulled out his book and notepad; the two people opening to chapter four.

Two hours passed by as Brie patiently went over the formulas and equations first. A unit circle was the easiest way for her to get the message across. When six p.m. drew closer, Brie told him about the extra problems at the back of the book she wanted him to work on for next week.

"Use the flash cards I gave you if you get stuck," she told him as she packed up her bookbag. He had to admit that the way Brie explained things, and her strategic methods made it easier to understand what was going on.

"Thank you, Brie," he said, staring at her, and she smiled warmly.

"You're welcome. Have a good weekend." Xander watched her walk away, noticing she had a nice, round behind.

****

The next morning had a brisk feel to it, and Xander's

girlfriend, Starr Strauss, had come over to the frat house to give him some pre-game action. The big game was in a few hours, and she knew giving Xander some nookie always relaxed him before he played. He was on his back, and she was bouncing up and down on him with vigorous movements. Starr liked being in charge in the bedroom, and she enjoyed this position because it allowed her to control things. She was naked from the waist down and only had on a blue, lace bra covering her breasts.

They had been dating for two years, and knowing that he was going to the NFL, Starr was going to hang onto Xander for dear life because she knew he'd be making a shitload of money once he went pro. Starr was a pistol in bed, and she moaned as her slow-building climax flowed over her in satisfying spasms.

Xander had no problem keeping her sexually satisfied, but she had needs that always had to be tended to. She had been good at keeping her other involvements a secret. As long as she played her role as a good girlfriend and got what she wanted as well, then everything would work out. She collapsed on his damp chest when Xander came, and they were breathing hard.

"That was awesome, babe," she commented, kissing his cheek. Starr was fair skinned with freckles sprinkled across her nose. She had a stylish haircut, a small forehead with a pointy chin, and small lips.

Xander was stroking her head, mentally preparing himself for the game later. They were playing their rival school tonight, and the crowds would be excited on both sides of the field.-Xander's room was rectangle in shape with a long twin bed on either side of the room. It was a typical guy room with posters of bikini models, a desktop computer, a sound system, and a black chest was at the foot of Xander's bed. It had two closets instead of drawers and was decorated in simple black and white.

"What are you thinking about?"

"Just thinking about the new plays tonight," he replied, and Starr rolled her eyes. She had never been into sports, but to be on Xander's arm and getting the notoriety of being his girl, she was going to fake it all the way to the top.

"You're going to bring home the victory, babe. I'm going to go so you can put your mind on the task at hand." Xander bunched the pillow under his head and watched her leave, feeling lucky to have a woman like Starr by his side. He knew she didn't prefer sporting events, but she dealt with it for him, and he was grateful that she was willing to tolerate something she wasn't interested in.

Xander's team ended up losing the game by three points, and even though the school had lost, Xander played a helluva game, and the scouts had been impressed. Through the rest of the semester, Brie continued to tutor Xander, and by the time December rolled around, his math grade had risen to an A, and he was overjoyed.

"You're doing so well, Xander. I see no reason for us to continue the sessions, especially since you've been keeping up your grade," Brie told him, playing with the end of her highlighter. It was two weeks before finals, and everyone was aching for winter break to begin.

"I can't tell you how much I appreciate all your help, Brie," he mentioned, giving her a high five. Over the last few months, they had become good friends, and it was strictly a companionable relationship.

"You don't have to thank me, Xander. Just keep doing

what you're doing."

"Well, I don't want this to be our last gathering. My fraternity is having an end of the year party with the Pi Mus. You should stop by tonight," Xander told her, and her face scrunched up.

"Frat parties aren't really my thing, Xander."

"They're not that bad, and it won't be all frat people there, Brie. It's just a chance for you to cut loose if you want to."

"Hmm... I'll think about it."

They talked for a few more minutes before they left their last study session. Brie tossed around Xander's invitation all day. She really wasn't the frat party type, but it might be interesting to see how it was. She easily found the Christmas-decorated address on the street that mostly held similar households.

She could hear "Super Freak" by Rick James blasting from the speakers and walked past the few people who were standing outside. Unzipping her coat, she looked around and saw people dancing, drinking, and talking. Pi Mu was mostly a Hispanic fraternity, so there was a mixture of people in the house.

Some had on green and red to celebrate the upcoming holiday, and there was even a guy dressed as Santa Claus going around kissing girls. Brie saw Xander's sweetheart standing in a corner talking to a guy, and she slowly moved around the big living room. She smiled when the Santa Claus gave her a peck on the cheek, and she bobbed her head to the side when "Let's Dance" by David Bowie started playing.

Brie managed to spot Xander walking toward the kitchen, and she headed that way. She decided to let him know she had just stopped by and then would leave. The hallway to the kitchen was long with hardwood floors that had garland lining the walls and had red glow sticks draping from the ceiling. She stopped when she heard some guys talking, pausing at the doorway.

"You invited your tutor? Why, man?"

"She's a good person. It's a party, right? So chill out."

"I'm just saying, she's a nerd. We don't need nerds at our party."

"She is a little cutie, though. I wouldn't mind private lessons from her." Xander shook his head at the comment from a Pi Mu guy, taking a sip of his wine cooler.

There were six guys standing in the kitchen talking, and some people were on the patio just beyond the room. Xander wasn't surprised they knew about Brie. They had been seen in several spots on campus, and they were always studying.

"C'mon, guys. Xander isn't interested in that girl when he has a lady like Starr. Right, Xander?"

Brie didn't hear Xander's response, and she felt her heart pounding in her chest. This is what one gets from overhearing conversations that weren't meant to be heard. Brie didn't see who Xander was talking to, but she didn't like the fact that he wasn't saying anything to stand up for her.

"What's her name?"

"Brie, and she's OK."

"Yeah, I bet.. She's the girl you hook up with and don't call the next day."

"Or you mess around with her and don't tell your friends. Geeks are hot in bed!" The guy who said that patted his friend on the back and let out a hearty laugh.

Xander chuckled at that, still not saying anything to the guys he was talking to. Brie left before they said anymore and not hear her so-called "friend" defend her. She understood guys talked about girls and vice versa, but the fact that Xander didn't even try to correct his moronic friends hurt the most. She had believed they were pals, but she was so wrong about that. The party was the last time they had been around each other, and the two ended up parting ways. Xander never thought about Brie again since he had graduated and went into the NFL, and she became focused on taking over the hotel…

Xander blinked and realized that twenty minutes had passed while he reminisced about his college time with Brie. He stood up and left the office after shutting off the computer; glad that she had agreed to join him for lunch.

Chapter 4

When Xander got to the restaurant, he saw Brie sitting in one of the booths near a window and joined her. He had easily obtained a cab and it took a few minutes for him to get there. He unbuttoned his jacket and sat back in the seat.

"I thought you forgot about our plans," she commented when he settled in and he shook his head.

"Sorry about that. Got held up at the office."

"Everything OK?" Brie wondered, and he gave a quick jerk of his head. Brie looked at him peruse the menu, thinking he had grown more handsome over the years. Of course, his facial features were older, but everything about him seemed to fit as far as an attractive male. He seemed more confident now, and he had an aura of authority when he entered the room.

"Have you ordered yet?"

"No, not yet. I was waiting for you. How long do you think the renovations will take?" Brie asked with her chin in her palm.

"It's hard to tell until we get in and see the layout."

"My dad said he would always get an estimate and would

pay half up front and the rest once the job was done. Is that staying the same?"

"Of course. We won't disrupt the usual business practices," Xander responded, and she sat back, clearing her throat.

"How many men do you have on your crew?"

"At least fifty. They get split up with the jobs we get commissioned with."

"Is your licensing and insurance up to date?"

Xander grinned an understandable smile before answering. "I see you're still by the book. And to answer your question, yes, they are. What are you ordering?"

"Chicken pasta. You?"

"Just a burger." Xander openly eyed Brie, thinking her features had softened over the years, and it looked like she laughed a lot. He liked how warm and welcoming her eyes were, and she had grown into a stunning woman.

"What happened to you in college, Brie?" Her eyebrows furrowed at that.

"What do you mean?" A server approached the booth with a pad and pencil in her hand, halting their conversation.

52

"Welcome to Del Prado's. My name is Stephanie. Can I start you off with something to drink?" Her eyes were on Xander, and Brie wasn't put off by it.

"Ladies first." Brie ordered a lemon water, and he ordered one as well.

"I see you haven't lost your touch with the ladies," Brie remarked, shifting in her seat. The eatery was busy from the lunch crowd, but it wasn't overly packed.

"Meaning?"

"Xander, you have to have known in school, as far as football went, you were the big man on campus, and all the girls wanted you." Brie informed him, and he drew back at that.

"Now you're exaggerating," he retorted, brushing her words away. Stephanie returned with their drinks, and they placed their orders.

"So you're not going to answer my question, Brie?"

"I'm still trying to understand what you mean."

"I invited you to a party, and you didn't show up. After that, we didn't talk anymore. I thought we were friends." Xander glanced at the people walking by the window, but he turned his attention back to Brie.

"Yeah, so did I. And I showed up at the house. I heard your friends talking about me, and you didn't defend me."

"What are you talking about?" When she spoke, Xander suddenly recalled the event and remembered the guys discussing her. His friends had talked about how she had a nice ass, but she was no Starr.

He hadn't said anything, not because he didn't want to but because it was harmless chat. In retrospect, Xander should've said something to the boneheads since Brie had been a nice person back then and didn't deserve their barbs.

"Brie… hell, I'm—"

"You don't have to apologize, Xander. It happened years ago. You wanted to know why we stopped talking, and that was the reason."

"No, I do have to make amends. You didn't do anything to deserve it, and I should've been a man and said something. I'm sorry, Brie." She took a sip of water and looked around the room. She wished this apology had come years ago, but it was over and done with. Brie didn't hold any ill feelings toward Xander about it.

"Brie? Nothing to say?"

"I accept your apology, Xander. We're going to be seeing a lot of each other due to the restorations, so let's just start over and retain a professional relationship," she answered him, and he agreed.

Brie took a deep breath, not knowing how his regret would affect her years later. She wasn't expecting it, and it felt like she had some type of closure. The waitress dropped off their food, and they ate a few bites in silence.

"Do you miss playing football?" she asked suddenly, and he looked up, startled by her question. It had been a minute since anyone talked to him about the sport as far as being a participant.

"I miss the excitement, the roar of the fans, and the traveling. My mom was happy when I retired. She didn't want me to do permanent injury to myself."

"That tackle you received that caused you to break both wrists… People still say it was a freak accident on the field."

Xander replayed that moment in his head like it had just happened. His team had just come from two Super Bowl wins back-to-back, and it was a regular season game. A big, bulky outside linebacker came from behind Xander and took him down as he executed the game winning play.

The way his wrist was positioned under his body when Xander hit the ground caused both of his wrists to break. Needless to say, he had never thrown the ball the same way again. Fortunately, he had a back-up plan with the construction company and became a successful businessman.

"Xander?" Brie saw the faraway look in his eyes, and she didn't mean for him to rehash old memories. "Are you all right?" He nodded and cleared his throat.

"I didn't mean to bring up bad times."

"You didn't. God just had a different plan for me, and I don't regret what happened." Their eyes met, and she grinned slightly.

"How are your parents?" Brie had never met them, but she knew from conversations with Xander in college his parents were strong proponents of him finishing school before joining the NFL.

"They're good. I bought them a house in Oak Brook. Mom wanted to be closer in case grandkids came about, and my dad can't say no to her."

"You have kids?"

"No, not yet. Starr isn't ready."

"Starr? You married Starr Strauss?" Xander's eyebrows went up at Brie's question due to the tone of it.

"Yes. We've been married for six years. What's with the tone?" he asked, taking a bite of his burger.

"No disrespect intended, but Starr wasn't the nicest person in college. I didn't know you two had gotten married." Brie finished her pasta and her water.

"She wasn't nice to you?"

"I overheard her snapping at some people from the drama club. I guess they must've accidentally bumped into her in the hall, and she went off on them."

"I'm sure she didn't mean it." Xander stopped himself from commenting further on Starr's behavior, especially given the state of their marriage. Brie was about to speak when two guys approached their table.

"Excuse us? Aren't you Xander Sterling?" the short one asked.

"Yes, I am."

"I told you! Can we have your autograph?" Brie watched

as Xander signed two napkins and smiled at them, patiently answering a few questions from the fans.

"Does that happen a lot?"

"Occasionally."

They spoke for a few more minutes and left after he paid the bill. They decided to share a cab back toward their destinations, and the taxi headed for the hotel first. As Brie was looking out the window, Xander took his time to observe her again.

He took sight of her smooth thighs that peeked from beneath her gray skirt when she crossed her legs. They gleamed like brown velvet under the afternoon sun, and her womanly figure was complemented by her ample breasts which were pressed against her pink blouse. He was glad their paths had crossed and was able to make amends for what went down years ago. Like she said, they would see a lot of each other, and it would be advantageous to have a fresh start between them.

****

Xander sauntered into his house in Frankfort, surprised to find it was empty. Starr had already been up and gone when he left for work that morning. It was a little after eight p.m., and she wasn't home yet. He saw a pot of spaghetti sauce with noodles sitting on the stove; still warm to the touch. They had hired a part-time maid to cook and clean, and this was a regular work day for her.

The house had a towering, arched, wooded door, which opened up into a grand entryway that allowed visitors to view the glass chandelier and ivory marbled tile in the parlor and living room. The dining room was down a long hallway with a rectangle-shaped table and eight chairs. The table sat in front of big, wide windows and a carpeted staircase that led to the four bedrooms and three baths upstairs. Xander knew this was a day that Ursula had prepared dinner. Starr could barely cook and was never interested in learning. After leaving Starr a voice message, Xander texted her, inquiring about her whereabouts and waited for a reply.

He ate dinner by himself then went upstairs to take a shower. Afterward, he got in the bed and turned on the big screen TV to the news with one leg bent with his back against the cushioned headboard. Xander thought back to Brie's comment about Starr. His parents hadn't been too happy when he married her, but they supported his decision and attended the ceremony with unnatural smiles. Xander's mom, Lola, didn't think Starr really loved her son and was just with him because of his money.

Before he got hurt and retired, Starr was an active and participatory wife. She was at all his home games, went out with him to all the sport related events, and even hung out with some of the other wives. He'd noticed a difference now that he wasn't in the game anymore. Starr went out a lot more with her best friend, Casey. She was barely home, and they hadn't had sex in months. Xander had talked to her about starting a family three months ago, and she had told him she wasn't ready yet.

Xander checked his phone and saw that she hadn't called back or responded to his text. He called Casey as well, but her phone went to voicemail. He looked at the clock and saw it was 9:37 p.m. He started to flip through the channels and decided to wait up for her. If she walked in after ten p.m., that was her ass.

****

Meanwhile, at an all-white party in a downtown

penthouse, Starr was having another orgasm from the man giving her head. A second guy, whose dick was in her mouth, grabbed her hair, and she opened it wider. She and Casey had gotten to the party six hours ago, and she was having the time of her life. Casey knew all the hot parties and people who could get them into the best gatherings.

The all-white party wasn't named for the dress code, but for the drugs that were supplied there. There was so much heroin and cocaine flowing around it looked like a winter wonderland. Starr had taken her fair share of ecstasy, and she had such a high it made her want to bounce on every dick in the room. She had lost count after being with five guys and two women.

The white man whose head was between her legs stood up, flipped her over and entered her without a condom. In addition to the drugs, weed was being smoked, there was a buffet of food, strippers were scattered around the room, some guys were playing video games, and there was a DJ. Amidst all the excitement, Starr had lost sight of Casey. The last time she saw her, she was riding some Italian guy on the couch. A different man stepped in front of Starr, and she smiled when she saw him unbuckling his pants.

****

Starr crept into the quiet house at one in the morning with her heels dangling from her fingertips. She made sure she looked presentable, even though Xander wouldn't be up. All she wanted was to take a long shower and go to bed. Starr jumped when the bedside lamp turned on and saw her husband glaring at her. Xander was clearly pissed, and she knew she had to do some major sweet-talking to soothe his feathers.

"You've been gone for over twelve hours! Where in the hell have you been, Starr?" he growled at her, his hands shaking from his anger.

"I was out with Casey," she said softly, strolling into the walk-in closet.

"All damn day!"

"Honey, I'm sorry. The time just got away from me. You know how it is when it's girl's night out."

"It's been girl's night out all fucking week!"

"Watch the potty mouth, Xander."

"Don't tell me what to do. I'm entitled to curse if my wife has been out all day!" Xander was seriously annoyed that Starr was nonchalant about coming home this late. Her ass could've been laid up in some hospital, and she didn't seem to care she had him worried.

Starr took off her white, fitted, sleeveless dress and walked toward him in a sexy strut. Although she was tired and sore, she'd give Xander some ass and a nice blow job. *That should distract him*, she said to herself.

"I'm sorry, babe. I didn't mean—" Xander stepped back when she tried to touch him on his chest.

"You stink, Starr," he said with disgust in his voice.

"Xander!"

He rolled his eyes and shook his head. "I'm going to bed."

She watched as he went to the California king and got under the covers. Starr let out a deep breath and walked to the bathroom without saying another word. The hot water was blasting, and it covered the mirror in a balmy fog. Starr swiped at it with a towel and stared at her reflection. At times, she could look at herself and be okay with what she saw. Ever since she accidently saw her dad's copy of *Hustler* magazine in his sock drawer at the age of thirteen, she had been curious about the human body and sexuality.

Starr knew her dad had kept loose dollar bills in his sock drawer, and she wanted some money so she could go to the candy store with her best friend. While shuffling through them, she saw the open pages where a white woman was posed fully naked. Her parents were entertaining the neighbors next door, so she knew she had time to examine and flip through the publication. She saw black, Asian, and Mexican women positioned in various ways, but they were all naked. She was able to see different sized bodies, and that made her curious about hers.

Later that night, she stared in the full-length mirror of her bedroom and took in her naked body. Of course, she had seen it before, but that was the first time she had touched herself. She played with her still-developing, small breasts and stared at her hairy girl area. Some of the ladies in the book had been hairy down there too, so she didn't feel bad. Starr spent the next year getting familiar with herself and would play between her legs with her fingers. She later realized that the images from the magazine were a trigger and she liked how it felt when she would have orgasms from her self-pleasure.

She decided that in her sophomore year to find out what

happened between a girl and a boy and ended up losing her virginity at fifteen to the captain of the swim team after hooking up at a party. After that, it seemed like the floodgates had been opened. She loved the feeling and excitement of sex and wanted it all the time. She had slept her way through the varsity swim and basketball team and didn't care about the reputation she had acquired. She was an easy lay, and most of the school knew it. When she wasn't fucking jocks, she had moved to guys in her regular classrooms, some band members, and a few boys on the yearbook committee.

When she couldn't get it from a male, she would watch porn and get off on that. During her senior year of high school, she had looked up sex addiction and read about the symptoms and treatment options. She also had read testimonies from sex addicts, and the majority said that they felt powerless over it. Starr felt the opposite and decided that nothing was wrong with her. If anything, she felt absolute powerful when she was screwing and getting her rocks off. She felt like a queen, and the guys she messed around with were just there to please her.

When she met Xander in college, Starr knew he was different when he didn't try to sleep with her on their first date.

He had been such a sweetheart, and it bothered her when she would cheat on him, but she couldn't stop herself then, just like she couldn't stop herself now. She stepped inside the shower and closed her eyes as the water streamed down her body. She would wait until later when Xander cooled down to talk to him to straighten things out.

Chapter 5

Brie sipped her hot tea as she was waiting on Xander, Marshall, and their foreman to arrive the next morning. She was standing at the front desk and glanced at her Blackberry. The desk clerk had just clocked in, and they greeted each other.

"Ms. Calhoun, I have to tell you, everyone is excited about the renovations to expand the hotel," Kate told her, and Brie smiled.

"I'm glad to hear that. This will be an improvement for the business and employees too. How is your husband and son?"

Kate smiled at the question. "They're fine. Bob is almost done with grad school, and Cecil is being a six-year-old."

Brie laughed at that part. "I know you're so proud of Bob."

"I am. We're going to party good when he graduates." Her husband was on the verge of completing his master's in psychology. Brie finished her drink, threw the cup away, and looked up when Marshall sauntered in with a tall white man.

"Good morning, Ms. Calhoun," Marshall said.

"Good morning, and call me Brie, please."

"This is our foreman, Doug Greenway." Marshall

introduced her to the man who wore a faded, plaid work shirt, old jeans, and was bald headed. He was clean cut and had a nice smile.

"Nice to meet you." Brie reached out and took the hand he offered; Doug shaking it with vigor.

"Same here. Thank you for this opportunity," Doug told her with a sparkle in his eyes.

"You're welcome. If you two want to grab some coffee or breakfast, you can put it on my tab at the restaurant."

They declined and talked until Xander walked in a few minutes later. He was wearing jeans, black boots and a black polo shirt with his company logo on it. Even though he was dressed in the same fashion as Marshall and Doug, Xander was the one who caught her eye.

"Good morning, Brie."

"Morning, Xander. Are you OK?" she asked in a concerned voice.

"Yes, why do you ask?"

"You look tired," she replied. Xander hadn't gotten much sleep after his conversation with Starr and woke up grouchy because he had tossed and turned all night. She was sleeping when he left that morning, and he didn't bother to wake her.

"I'm fine. Let's just get this walk-through over with." Marshall looked at Xander from the manner of his words and wondered what was up with him. They walked a few feet next door to the abandoned building, and Brie gave Doug the key.

"Here you go, Brie." Marshall gave her a hard hat, and she thanked him.

They entered the building, and she was hit with the smell of mold and mildew. There was minimal light from the covered windows, and she could hear water dripping with creatures scurrying about. The three guys pulled out flashlights and decided to start from the top and work their way down. Brie was quiet as they made notes in their binders and talked amongst themselves.

The building they were in was only ten stories tall, so they would have to add to the structure that was already in place to match the level of the hotel. Brie went to look out through the cracks of a boarded-up window, and Xander glanced at her. He knew he'd have to apologize for his earlier mood.

She was the client, and she shouldn't have been the target of his anger toward Starr. He noticed how snug her jeans were across her behind, which was pleasantly plump. They made it down to the first floor, and Brie couldn't keep quiet anymore.

"Well? How is everything?"

"The foundation looks good, but I'm going to come back tomorrow and do a stress test. I'm also going to check for damage like any past flooding issues, termites, and asbestos. The good thing is it matches the width of your hotel, so we won't have to dig. As we go up each floor, we're going to have to knock down each wall to connect the hotels," Doug explained, looking at his notes.

She crossed her arms and looked at the three men. "I was thinking about that last night. I only want to connect the first three floors and have this building be Tower B."

"Are you sure?" Xander inquired.

"Yes. It seems better to have two separate buildings," she answered.

"OK, we'll have to look at the plans again and revamp them." They left the dim dwelling, and Brie squinted against the sunlight as she gave the hard hat to the foreman.

"I'm going to head to the office and get things started. The guys finished the Naperville job, so we'll have all hands-on deck for this project," Doug told the bosses before he left the group.

"When will the job start?"

"In about two days. First, we'll have to gut the building, and we'll take care of the disposal," Xander answered her question, and Brie noticed his disposition seemed to have gotten better from their earlier greeting.

"Do you have some more plans or ideas for the building?" Marshall asked as they walked back into the lobby.

"No, just as long as the buildings are the same length and similar design."

"Not a problem. We're going to have our architect draw up final plans and bring them back here this afternoon. Is three a good time?"

"No. I have a consultation for a sweet-sixteen party at that time. How about four p.m.?"

Marshall nodded at that. "Good. See you at four." Brie walked toward the elevators and Marshall glared at Xander.

"What the hell is wrong with you, man? Why were you rude to her?" he demanded once she was out of earshot, and Xander sighed.

"Let's go," he said marching out, giving Marshall no choice but to follow him.

****

Once they were behind closed doors at the office, he told him about the night before, and Marshall's eyebrows raised in shock when Xander explained Starr's behavior. He could understand his friend being in a funky mood today after hearing what happened.

"Where was she for all those hours?" Marshall asked his buddy, who was tapping a pencil on his desk.

Xander shrugged at the question. "I don't know. She never told me."

"You're better than me. I wish Natalie would walk up in the house at one in the morning after being gone all damn day." Natalie was Marshall's wife, and they were ridiculously devoted to one another.

"That'll never happen since you two are joined at the hip." Marshall's facial expression acknowledged that statement. He could see that Xander was hurting, frustrated, and concerned at the same time. All Marshall could do was listen, offer advice, and be a friend. If Xander listened to it, that would be a different story.

"Listen, X, Starr is your wife, and I know you love her. But some things are unacceptable, and what she did was one of them. You should wait until you've cooled down, then talk to her. You also need to apologize to Brie for this morning. You can't take your anger out on a client, man. You know I have your back, but you gotta leave that personal stuff at the door. This is a big opportunity for the company, and we can't let anything screw it up. We have to be professional going forward."

Xander rubbed his hand across his chin and exhaled, silently agreeing with his words. "You're right. I will talk to her this afternoon."

"Good. Let's take a minute and then come together to finalize things for the project," Marshall suggested before leaving Xander's office. He knew his business partner was right about some things; he did need to calm down before trying to talk to Starr. He was going to find out where she was, even if he had to take the polite route.

Starr had texted him to see if he could meet her for lunch, but he declined her offer. He wasn't ready to sit down with her

73

and pretend like everything was fine. He let out another deep breath and put his focus towards the task at hand. He didn't bother to admit that a small part of him perked up at the thought of seeing Brie twice in a day.

Hours later, Brie was slowly walking from the Lotus banquet room, making notes on the clipboard she had for the meeting with Ross Overstreet. He was the head of the PR department for the United Center. His daughter was turning sixteen, and he was going all out. He had reserved the room months ago and wanted to meet with Brie and the party planner.

His daughter wanted a fire and ice theme, which was fine with Brie as the concept was laid out by the planner. She was all for the idea to make the birthday party special for the teenager, but she put her foot down on a fire performer doing a set during the celebration. She placed the clipboard on the front desk to finish her notes as steady activity was going on around her. People were coming and going, women were entering the spa, and the buzz from the restaurant could be heard.

"Hi, Brie." She looked up and saw Xander standing close

to the desk.

"Hey, Xander. Is it four already?" She looked at the clock on her phone and saw it was five past the hour.

"Are you done with your meeting?"

"Yes, I was just finishing up. Is Marshall with you?"

"He's on the way," he responded.

"Great. We can head up to my office. Can you let him know to come up to the third floor?"

"Yeah, I'll just shoot him a text," he mumbled, following her toward the elevators.

Entering the office, Xander liked the space, noting it had good lighting, and he also liked how her clothing fitted her.

"You mind if I get comfortable?" Brie asked, sitting behind her desk.

"No, go ahead." He sat down on the sofa, watching her take her jacket off. Brie had changed into a navy-blue skirt with a white blouse for the meeting.

"How was your day?" she asked as she was shuffling her feet under the desk.

"It was good. Thanks for asking." Xander was thrown off by her question. It had been a while since a woman, besides

75

his mother, had asked how his typical day was. Starr certainly hadn't inquired in quite some time. She smiled at him and stepped from behind the desk wearing red, fuzzy socks. Xander chuckled at her footwear as she wiggled her toes.

"I'm relaxed, Xander," she said in a light, defensive voice.

"I can tell," he replied with a grin, unrolling a set of blueprints he had with him. He was quiet as she looked over the plans he had laid out. She liked how the second building was designed, and he patiently answered her questions.

"There will be at least twenty guys to help with the clean out and then we'll go from there."

"Do you help too?" she asked, looking at him over her left shoulder.

"Yes, I'll jump in when help is needed." Brie was quiet as she perused the plans again. Her scent wafted over him, and it was a mixture of lavender and jasmine. Although it was an unusual combination, it complimented her.

He looked down at his chirping cell phone. It was a text message from Marshall, notifying Xander to continue the meeting without him since he was still stuck on a conference call.

"Marshall won't be able to join us."

"Oh, no problem. Everything looks good, and the lawyers said the contract you sent over appears fine. What's the total cost?" she questioned in a steady voice.

He laid out the rate and included the labor, and after he showed her the final price, she went back to her desk and phoned the accounting department to let them know how much to write a check for. It was located on the second floor, and it was a two-person operation.

"The check should be here in a few minutes. Would you happen to know any good landscapers?

"We have a company we consult with. Why?"

"I want to add another fountain to go outside the new building," she replied.

"You're looking to improve this place to the max, I see." He watched her lean back; the colorful socks a contrast to her professional attire.

"I want this hotel to be one that's on the tourist's minds and the city can be proud of. When people come to visit Chicago, I want it to be their first choice, hands down," Brie stated with so much conviction, Xander wanted to stand up and applaud her. As a businessman, he could appreciate her drive to succeed.

"I feel you, Brie. You have a vision for the hotel, and there's nothing wrong with that. I realize you want to make sure everything is on point with the hotel."

"I want to thank S&T for helping me achieve it. I feel like the renovations will help with that, and we won't have to turn people away because we're booked."

"Does that happen a lot?"

"No, not often. We've had a few, but I don't want to continue that pattern. You know what I mean?"

Brie liked talking shop with another business owner. Because she was at the hotel most of the time, a lot of her conversations centered around the guests and employees. Brie admitted she was a workaholic and yearned for an identity outside the hotel, so she could be someone other than a hotel owner. There was a short knock on the door, and Brie opened it for the head accountant, Samuel, who handed her an envelope.

"I know exactly what you mean," Xander responded as she handed him the check.

Xander placed it in his wallet and made a mental note to deposit it into the company bank account once he left. His eyes latched onto hers, and he struggled to pull them away.

"Can I get a tour of the place?" he asked suddenly, and Brie was surprised by his question. Xander had changed since this morning as well. He had on khakis and a baby-blue polo shirt. It was stretched across his muscles, and that color matched well against his skin. She put her heels back on, and they departed the office.

Ms. Darla had left, and they took the elevator up to the top floor. Brie was glad when the doors opened. Xander's cologne had surrounded the space, and she needed to not be near it. Not because it smelled bad... no, it was far from that. It was a leathery, oaken scent, and she liked it.

Brie showed him one of the empty suites, and he was impressed by what he saw with the space, furniture, and decorations. The windows at each end of the halls were sealed and had great views. Oil and abstract paintings adorned the walls, and some hall tables held fresh hydrangeas in glass vases. She proceeded to show him the daycare, business center, fitness room, both pools, and the spa.

"The restaurant pays you rent?" He probed, seeing how busy it was from the doors in the lobby.

"Yes. It wasn't part of the original design, and the owner saw potential by the high clientele we get here." The tour had ended, and they sat on the cushioned, low-back chairs across from the check-in desk.

"Very impressive, Brie."

She smiled and tilted her head at his words. "Thank you. I can't wait to see how the building will look once it's done."

"I know the guys are excited. Anything that keeps them working makes them happy."

"Is there ever a slow time with construction?" Since things were calm right now, Brie could focus on the conversation with Xander.

"It's slow during the winter months. That's why we like to have enough jobs when the weather is nice," Xander responded to the question in a relaxed tone.

They spoke for a few more minutes, then he stood up to leave.

"Take care, Brie."

"You too, Xander."

"Are you leaving to go home?" he asked softly.

"No, I have some more work to do. I'll probably leave here around eight or nine."

"Don't work too hard." Brie chuckled at that, and Xander liked the sound. She told him goodnight, and he watched as she strode through the lobby. Turning on a sigh, Xander left the place and headed for the bank as soon as he got in his car.

****

Starr looked at the candlelit dinner that was placed on the dining room table and smiled with approval. Xander would be home any minute, and she needed everything to be perfect. He still wasn't talking to her, and she wanted to fix things. Casey had called her about another party tonight, but she declined. She wanted to go, but she had to fix things with her husband.

It was the maid's day off, so she had called and had dinner delivered, and Starr was glad she did. The delivery guy was Jamaican and was hot as hell. After she gave him a tip, they made small talk before having a quickie in the hallway. It didn't even bother her that Xander might've shown up at the same time the guy was hitting it from the back against the banister. Just thinking about it make Starr hot, and she started to throb between her legs.

She hated cheating on Xander, but she had an obsession that needed to be fed. Starr had secretly seen a doctor a few years before and was diagnosed with a sexual addiction. Of course, she didn't tell Xander, and she was careful during the first few years of their marriage by carrying condoms. But lately, she'd been consumed by the sexual thrill, and it was causing her to do what she could to get her release.

Starr knew being a sex addict didn't justify her infidelities, but she didn't know how to stop it. She heard the garage door open, and she rushed to turn on the radio to an easy listening station. She had on skin-tight, black shorts with an emerald blouse. Earlier, she had gone to get a manicure and pedicure and got her hair done. It was cut into a stylish bob, and she hoped Xander liked it.

"Hi, honey," she said as he walked in through the kitchen, giving him a kiss on his cheek.

"Hey." She noticed he was still short with her and decided to push on with her plan.

"I have dinner waiting for you. I thought it would be nice for us to talk." She led him to the dining area, and he saw the setup. Xander sat down, and she poured them a glass of wine to go with the steak meal. He sniffed the liquid, raised it in a silent salute, and took a swallow. *So far so good*, Starr thought.

"What did you do today?" he asked as she uncovered the food; the inviting smells making his stomach growl since he hadn't eaten anything since lunch hours ago.

"I went to get my nails done and then to the hair shop." Xander sat back in his chair, watching Starr cut her food. If she thought he was going to forget about last night, she had another thing coming.

"Anything else?" She shook her head as she ate a piece of the porterhouse meat.

"You ready to tell me where you were last night?" he asked, holding onto the fork with a firm grasp.

"I told you. I was with Casey."

"Yeah, I got that part. What I didn't get was an answer. So let me ask you again. Where *were* you?"

Starr licked her lips and cleared her throat. "Honey, we're having such a nice dinner. Let's talk about something else."

"No! You got me looking like a damn fool, waiting up for

83

my own wife to come home. And you don't seem to care that your conduct is putting a wall between us."

"What conduct, Xander?" Starr was trying her best to steer him away from the discussion, but it wasn't working, and Xander hated when she played dumb.

"This isn't the first time you've come in late and not tell me where you were. You are always out with Casey and—"

"She's my best friend."

"She's a hoe."

"Xander!"

"Why do you think Gary divorced her? She couldn't keep her legs closed. Is that what you're doing? Are you fucking around on me?" Xander inquired with such hostility that Starr grimaced. She let out a deep breath, knowing she was about to lie and hoped she was convincing.

"Xander, I wouldn't do that. I love you, and I love our life together."

"I don't believe you!" He hissed as he threw the utensil down and left the room. Starr exhaled and drank the rest of her wine. Things didn't go as she expected, and a part of her was upset she had turned down Casey's offer to go out tonight. If she'd known he was going to act like that, she could've at least gone out and had a good time. Doing so probably would've added to the strife between them, but Starr was getting to the point where she didn't care. She figured she'd let Xander cool off before trying to approach him again.

Chapter 6

It was five days into the construction job, and so far, everything was going well. The workers were on the fourth and fifth floors gutting out the building. There was a truck parked in the alley to haul away the debris and trash. Radios had been setup and were playing different stations while the guys worked. The wooden boards had been removed from the windows, and with lanterns set up in various areas, it provided enough light for them to work. It was after nine a.m., and Brie walked into the construction site with two boxes of pastries and a container of coffee.

"Hello?" Brie called up the stairs but couldn't be heard over the music. She walked up the steps, mindful of the cords on the floor.

"Good morning!" Brie yelled once she cleared the landing. Doug looked up and saw her wave with a free finger.

"Ms. Calhoun, what are you doing here?" He relieved her of the boxes and placed them on a makeshift table.

"I bought breakfast for everyone," she answered, placing the coffee box down.

"Hold on, let me go get the bosses."

Doug headed upstairs, and she looked around for a minute then began to set things up after waving to the guys on the floor. Xander and Marshall came downstairs wearing hard hats, and Brie noticed that Xander was wearing a blue tank top with worn jeans. Of course, there were sweat stains on his shirt, but the way his muscles were glistening, and how his well-toned arms filled out the top, Brie found it very hard to look away from him. *Get a grip, girl. He's a married man!*

"Good morning, guys."

"Brie, you shouldn't be in here without a hard hat on; it's against code," Xander expressed, looking at her. It was hard to reprimand Brie when she had on a yellow pantsuit, and it made her look like a splash of sunshine.

"I'm leaving. I just bought food for all the guys."

"You didn't have to do that," Marshall stated, looking over the spread.

"It's no problem. Everyone has been working so hard, I wanted to show my thanks and spark some energy in the process," she explained, looking at both men, but her eyes kept gravitating toward Xander. Brie left on that note, and Xander went with her to make sure she got out safely.

"Thank you again for the food," Xander told her as they were standing outside the building.

"You're welcome. I'll be out for the rest of the day. My executive assistant manager will be around, but if you need anything, you can call me."

"OK, have a good one." She waved, and Xander couldn't help but watch her walk away. He liked that color on her, and the way her hips swayed. She looked the part of a business owner, and he appreciated her curves. But he was a married man, and all that he could and would be was a friend and associate with Brie.

****

"I'm going to need you to be a little bit more excited by your blind date tonight," Faith remarked as Brie was looking at her new hairdo in the mirror. Her friend had arranged an entire day of pampering for Brie, who hardly ever took time for herself. She had gotten her ends clipped, and her hair now flowed with honey-colored highlights. She also had gotten a lemon-scrub pedicure with a bright-pink hue and clear coat on her fingernails that had been shaped. It had been a while since she had been pampered like this and was enjoying it.

Faith had finished filming her movie and was heading home to North Carolina but had to switch planes in Chicago, due to an engine problem. She had a three-hour layover and could've easily taken another private jet, but she wanted to spend time with Brie and Qyle. The latter was sitting in a cushioned chair being a spectator, thumbing through an outdated magazine. She absolutely hated this girly stuff and only went for her friends.

"I am excited," she responded in a bland tone, looking at her gorgeous friend. Brie could understand why the camera loved Faith and why she graced the cover of so many magazines. Even in jeans and a shirt, she was still a beauty yet humble at the same time.

"But your date is with an aide to the deputy mayor, Brie." Faith's tone made it seem like this date was the best thing in the world, and Brie would get a feel for it once she met with Ike tonight.

"OK..." Faith rolled her eyes, sitting back in the chair next to Qyle.

"How did you meet anyway?" Qyle asked, looking up from the periodical.

"We met months ago. The mayor had hosted a luncheon at the restaurant, introductions were made, and somehow, I got in the mix. Because we're so busy, we've just been playing phone tag and talking over email."

"Where is he taking you for the date?"

"Just to Welsh's. It's a neutral point."

Faith walked over to Brie, who draped an arm around her shoulders. "It's going to be an awesome time tonight."

Brie smiled and patted her arm. "It sucks you have to leave so soon."

"I know, but we'll all get together soon and have a wine night… well in Qyle's case, a beer night." Qyle saluted at that, and they all chuckled.

****

Exactly fifty-one minutes after her date began, Brie was walking through the lobby of the hotel. She waved at the security guard and stopped at the front desk to retrieve her messages. Disaster… no, obnoxious was the word to describe the date. First, he was twenty minutes late and didn't call to let her know. When he finally showed up, he had the nerve to try to order for her, and he literally would not stop talking! My big house this… my cars that… my country club this…

"Brie?" She turned around and saw Xander heading her way. He had on black slacks with a gray V-cut shirt under a blazer.

"Oh, hey, Xander. What are you still doing here?"

"Waiting on Marshall and his wife. We decided to try out the restaurant here."

"Oh, good. Make sure you try the chocolate éclair cake. It's so delicious."

Speaking of delicious… Xander's eyes trickled down her shape, and he liked what he saw. A lot. She was wearing a periwinkle, form-fitting, spaghetti-strapped dress with a matching clutch and heels.

"Are you heading out?"

"No, coming in. I had a blind date."

"Oh, yeah? How was it?"

"You see I'm back early." He laughed, noticing the clock on the front desk showed 7:58 p.m.

"That bad, huh?" He grinned at her exaggerated head nod and eye roll and found that cute as hell.

"Yes, it was bad. I left before we could order." She had

her right elbow resting on the desk, her body turned his way. With her heels on, her eyes were leveled with his lips, and they looked soft to her.

"I'm sorry. That sounded like a nightmare," Xander told her, and she grinned sincerely.

"Thanks. It's not your fault."

"What are you going to do now?"

"Go up to my office and do some paperwork," she responded, her eyes bouncing between his dark eyes and lips.

Xander shook his head at her plans. "You can't waste a good night like this sitting in your office. Come and have dinner with us. You'll get a chance to meet Marshall's wife," Xander offered, and Brie was taken aback by the suggestion, knowing she would decline.

"Thank you for the invitation, Xander, but I don't want to intrude on your dinner plans."

"Intrude? Nah. You'd actually be saving me from having to watch them make googly eyes at each other. It's only going to be the three of us. You can even the group out."

Brie let out a deep breath, looking at her former classmate. "It honestly sounds like it's a couples thing only. Isn't Starr

92

coming?"

Xander shrugged and checked his phone again. Of course, there was no contact from her. She knew about dinner tonight, but she hadn't been home when he got there and hadn't returned his calls and messages. She was doing the same old shit, and he was tired of it.

"Apparently not. You'd be doing Natalie a favor by having another woman there. I know she's not going to like us guy talking." Xander pointed out in a convincing tone, and she chewed on her bottom lip while shuffling her feet.

"I don't know, Xander. Marshall and his wife might not want me to tag along." She returned, and he cocked his head to the side.

"If I ask them and they don't mind, will you join us?" he asked urgently. Xander didn't want to part from her yet, and Brie was somewhat glad he was pushing for her attendance.

"You're persistent tonight. Alright, but only if they say yes."

"Cool. You haven't eaten yet… we're going to dinner. It makes sense," he stated as Marshall and Natalie strolled in. Xander waved at them, and Brie walked alongside him as she went to greet the couple.

****

Meanwhile, Starr was in the midst of being double penetrated by two guys she didn't know when she was supposed to be at the dinner date. Casey had told her about a mansion in Elk Grove Village that was notorious for having wild sex parties, and that's what was going on when they arrived. Things had changed between her and Xander. They were having only polite conversation around the house, and they still weren't having sex. Starr needed that euphoria that came from intercourse. She vowed that she would make things right with her husband after tonight. As soon as she and Casey walked into the house and Starr saw all the decadent, sexual things going on, she immediately felt a hammering sensation between her legs. Her mind wasn't on Xander or the outing she was missing as she was relishing in the dual pummeling she was receiving.

Across town, Brie was glad Marshall and Natalie hadn't minded her tagging along on their dinner date, and she liked Natalie from the start. Natalie was shorter than Marshall with dread locs that were styled in a bun on top of her head. She was a high-school math teacher, and they had been married for seven years. Brie had just heard the story of how Marshall and Xander became friends after the former transferred to their school in his senior year. Their friendship had been solidified when they pledged the same fraternity and when Marshall joined the football team. They were drafted for the same NFL team, and he had played the tight-end position. Marshall ended up getting hurt a year before Xander, and once his contract had expired, he decided to leave that part of him behind.

"It's great that you two went into business together," Brie said before she took a sip of wine.

"I practically had to bully them to do it." Natalie informed, and Brie smiled at that, glancing at Xander.

"Yes, darling. You did have a hand in our decision." She lightly slapped his shoulder at his tone, and he winked at her. Natalie scooted her chair closer to Brie so they could girl talk. For a Friday night, as expected, the restaurant was busy. They ended up getting a good table in the middle of the room. There was enough space between each table where conversations could be private and not intruded upon. The environment was welcoming and pleasant.

It had a décor of burnt-orange walls, wooden tables, and chairs with Brazilian Cherry floors. The tables had white tablecloths and small, oval vases with low-cut, fresh flowers placed in them. The lights in the ceiling were in an arch design to provide even light in the restaurant. The bar was small but efficient, and it allowed more room for eating.

"So you and Xander were college friends?"

"Yes. I was his tutor."

"I bet he was the big man on campus, huh?"

"Something like that," Brie answered with a low chuckle. In addition to the main dish, they had ordered stuffed baby mushrooms as the appetizer.

"I love your hair. How long have you been growing it out?"

Natalie grinned, touching the twists. "Thank you. Since I was fifteen years old. I love that dress; it's a cute color."

"Thanks. I had a date tonight that didn't end well."

"Ugh! I don't miss those days," Natalie mentioned, eyeing Marshall, who was talking to Xander.

"Yeah, it's hard dating nowadays. You two are a cute

couple."

"Thank you," Natalie replied with a smile. "I'm glad you joined us tonight, Brie."

"I wasn't sure if you'd be OK with me coming along." Brie was having a good time hanging out with the Thorntons. Natalie was fun to talk to, and Brie could see a new friendship developing.

"Girl, please, any friend of Xander's is a friend of ours. Besides, you're way more fun than that wife of his. I can't stand her!" Brie peeked at Xander to make sure he hadn't overheard Natalie's words.

"Is that right?"

"Oh yeah. Starr never tries to converse when we get together, and she walks around like she's better than everyone. Starr just seems fake to me." Brie took in what Natalie was saying. She had those same feelings about Starr in college, but she was Xander's wife, so she had to have some good qualities.

The four-way conversation started back up, and between the laughs and easy camaraderie, Xander forgot about Starr not being there. He was having a good time knowing Brie was playing a part in that. She balanced out being his dinner companion with Marshall and Natalie, and he was glad she had agreed to it. When the women got up to go to the restroom, Marshall looked over his shoulder to make sure they had gotten out of earshot.

"I see the look you're giving Brie." Marshall reported to his friend, who scrunched his face.

"What look?" Xander asked, taking a drink of water. He knew what Marshall was getting at, but he didn't know that it was evident to his best friend. He'd just have to do a better job of masking whatever he was feeling for Brie.

"You're looking at her how I look at Natalie, and we both know what that leads to," Marshall stated, and Xander rolled his eyes.

"I'll admit that Brie is beautiful and smart. We're just friends.. I'm married, and we both respect that."

"I know. You'd never cheat on Starr, but you need to rein in those looks, man. We work for her now, so chill out."

Marshall was right. Not only was it inappropriate since she was their client but he wasn't the type of man to check out other women while married. He knew he was doing more than ogling Brie, but sometimes, he couldn't help it. She was an awesome woman, and he was glad they had reconnected. Later, after dinner was over, Xander replayed the evening in his mind as he drove home, and Brie did the same thing while sitting in her chair in her office with the lights off, looking at the darkness over the lake. The evening turned out not to be a complete failure, and she was able to know more about Xander. In her book, that was a win-win situation.

****

Brie had closed the dryer door when she heard Qyle come into her home. It was a Sunday evening, and it was a weekend she had off. She had cleaned her house earlier by mopping, dusting, and vacuuming, and was now washing clothes. She and Qyle had given each other spare keys to their places in case something happened. She came out the laundry room to see Qyle place a pizza box on the table.

"You still washing?"

"Yeah, I got a late start at it. How was your trip?"

"Good… in more ways than one." Qyle grabbed a beer bottle from the fridge, and they went to sit in the living room; the TV showing *Silence of the Lambs*.

"Do I even want to know what that means?"

"The negotiations with Extreme Striker went well. I went to a few clubs and got laid."

Brie nodded with her lips pinched. "Good to know," she said, reaching for the food.

"The date didn't work out, huh?" Qyle wondered as she grabbed a slice of pizza.

"No. He was the absolute worst. But I ended up having dinner with Xander, Marshall, and his wife." Brie recalled the evening with a serene grin, and Qyle stared at her. It was a smile of contentment that Qyle hadn't seen in a long time. Not that Brie shouldn't be smiling like that but not toward the company she was keeping. Qyle knew about their college history and that he was a married man.

"Was Xander's wife there?"

"Nope. She didn't show up."

"So you're pushing up on her man, huh? Qyle grinned and ducked when Brie flung a throw pillow at her. "I'm kidding. But seriously, do you like Xander?"

"Of course I do. I liked him in college too. We just have a professional relationship. It's not a big deal," Brie proclaimed.

She said it more for her own benefit than anything. She didn't want to hear Qyle's mouth about having feelings for him. Did she find Xander attractive? Yes. Was there a part of her that was feeling him on a personal level? Yes. But as long as she kept reminding herself that he was married, and they were friends, it would be fine. Brie knew she was sounding like a broken record, but she had to stay diligent on this matter.

Chapter 7

Starr and Casey were sitting at the dining room table of Starr's house, eating a bowl of popcorn, and playing with a deck of cards. Casey was a tall, white woman with long, blonde hair and double-D cup breast implants. The two women had started hanging out when their husbands were playing pro ball, and she had liked how Casey did things as far as the parties she attended and the people she hung out with.

When her husband, Gary, divorced her for cheating, Casey didn't seem fazed by it. The women remained friends after all these years, and she was always excited about what Casey would get her into. Xander was in the basement working out in his weight room. There was a treadmill, a wall ball, weight bench, and barbells that he utilized. It was two days after the dinner date Starr missed, and they needed to have a serious conversation.

"He's still not speaking to you?" Casey guessed, and Starr nodded her head. Since it was Sunday, they usually went to dinner at Xander's parents' house. However, since they weren't talking and Xander's mother didn't like Starr, she was fine with staying home.

"I'm so glad I'm not married anymore. I don't have to answer to anyone and can come and go as I please," Casey mentioned, holding a handful of popcorn.

"I love Xander, Casey," Starr said in a defensive tone.

"I'm not saying you don't. I'm just thinking it must be stressful trying to be a wife and seeing to your personal needs." Starr sighed at her best friend's words.

In a normal, loving marriage, the people involved would seek out each other for their own needs. It seemed easy for Casey to say because she didn't care about cheating on her husband. When Gary found out and divorced her, he had given her an undisclosed amount of money and was still living off that, in addition to the funds she got from the guys she was sleeping with.

When Xander came downstairs after taking a shower, Starr looked at him, not knowing that he had come up from the basement. He was dressed in jeans, a red T-shirt, and matching Jordans. Without saying anything to her, he grabbed his wallet and keys and left the house. Starr let out a deep breath and felt bad for the wall that was getting thicker between them.

"I have something to tell you that might cheer you up," Casey told Starr, sitting back in the chair with a smirk on her face.

"What's that?"

"I heard from a friend that there is a party being planned for the 4th of July on a boat."

"A boat?" Starr asked, her interest piqued.

"Well, a small yacht. It's a Mandingo party. You in?" Starr's innards jumped at the word, and she nodded. That news did indeed perk her up, and she was looking forward to the holiday.

****

Xander pulled up in his parents' house in the suburbs, and as soon as he stepped inside, his stomach rumbled at the aroma of his mother's cooking. He was glad he had come to see his folks. He could talk to his dad about Starr and hopefully get some much-needed advice. The house had just enough room for them and some overnight guests. Xander thought his parents should have a bigger home, but they were fine with what they had.

Walking into the roomy kitchen with white appliances, he stopped short when he saw his parents in a passionate embrace. They were leaning against the counter, and their arms were wrapped around each other. His dad's hands were snaked around his mother's behind, and he instantly cleared his throat when he saw his mom being groped.

"Didn't we take your key?" Xander's father, Xen, asked without preamble, and his mother, Lola, hit his shoulder before moving towards the stove.

"No," he replied on a chuckle.

"Damn, we need to. You interrupted my groove, son,"

"Don't pay your father any mind, dear. You're just in time for dinner. Where's Starr?" Lola asked, taking the steaming chicken breast out the oven.

"At home," he simply answered and went to wash his hands. Xen and Lola gave each other a look, and he shook his head with a shrug. Xen was a retired firefighter, and Lola was an author. She wrote mystery books, and her last one had sold thirty million copies. A hearty dinner of jerk chicken breast, steamed veggies, and cornbread had been served at the dining room table after his father had said grace.

"What's been going on with you?" Lola asked her son, picking up her utensils.

"We got charged with building the add-on to Dynasty Towers. The guys are thrilled because it's giving us work for a few months."

"That swanky hotel downtown?" Xander nodded as he chewed his food.

"That must be exciting," she replied. Xander went on to tell them about Brie and their college connection, and his dad looked surprised.

"Wow. Talk about small world, huh?"

"So Xander, why didn't Starr come with you?" Lola asked casually, ignoring the look Xen gave her.

"I really don't want to talk about it, Ma."

They finished eating with easy conversation, and when dinner was over, Xander asked to speak to his dad in private.

"Don't be too long, I have caramel cake for dessert," Lola informed the duo as they headed downstairs to the basement. It was the perfect man cave for Xen that had recliner seats, a big TV, full bathroom, one of those old-school jukeboxes, and a popcorn machine.

"She's going to make me doughy in the middle with all her cooking," Xen mentioned as he sat on a barstool, and Xander took a seat on the couch.

"You've been saying that for years, Dad." Xen shrugged and looked at his son. He sensed something was troubling him at the table, but he could wait until Xander was ready to talk. Xander didn't say anything for a few minutes, and Xen looked at him with concerned eyes.

"What's going on, son? Is everything OK?"

"Yes, I'm fine. I just need your advice about something." Xander told his dad what was going on with Starr; about her being gone all day and night, not answering her phone, and being evasive.

Xen blew out a breath while massaging his left palm with his right thumb, and Xander knew that move meant his father was thinking. He had seen that too many times while growing up and now welcomed it.

"You know Lola and I never liked Starr from the beginning, but you love her, and we respect that. But her behavior… don't tolerate it, son. Until she starts talking and gives you answers, take drastic measures. Take her off the bank account. I bet she starts speaking then."

"Dad!"

"I'm serious, Xander. If the tables were turned, you know Starr would hit you where it hurts. I'm not saying it to be vindictive, but there's no way she should be staying out all night and not telling you where she is. And you said it has been like this for the last six months?"

"The last eight months." Xander corrected, and Xen shook his head.

"Do you think she's cheating on you?"

Xander let out a deep breath and rubbed the back of his head. He didn't want to face the answer, but he wasn't going to lie to his dad either.

"Honestly, I do. I didn't want to say anything because I didn't want to admit that my marriage had failed," Xander proclaimed in a low voice, prompting his father to sit next to him. Xen patted his son on his knee and looked in Xander's eyes.

"Listen to me, son. First, get proof if you believe it. Second, if Starr is cheating on you, it doesn't reflect you. She's the one breaking your marriage vows. Don't let her actions cause you to doubt yourself as a husband. We raised an honorable man, and if she can't see that, she doesn't deserve you. Marriage is a lot of things, and one of them is making the union happy and content. If Starr is doing dirt, trust me, it'll come to light." Xen informed Xander, who let out a jerky nod.

He felt better after talking to his father. He was right about one thing: if Starr was doing dirt, it would indeed come to light. He didn't feel bad that his feelings were changing toward his wife since he was the one putting forth the effort. He tried to get her talking to him, and she was the one who was keeping tight-lipped about everything. Xander would give her a few months to change her behavior or that was it. He thanked his father, and they went back upstairs to enjoy Lola's homemade cake.

****

Brie was in the office, hunched down going through the employee file cabinet. She was pulling out those charts who had to go for a random drug test and get their annual TB shot done. It had been a month since the renovations started, and everything was going according to schedule. Most of the building had been gutted out, and she had seen some other trucks and material arrive last week.

She pulled out twelve files and went to the computer to print out a reminder letter to those staff members and sent an email to the department supervisors to make sure they followed up with the memo. Brie stood up and let out a good stretch by raising her arms above her head. She had gotten a lot done since arriving that morning and felt good about the dent she put in her work. She had gone through the guests' survey cards and added the compliments to the website. The three bad reviews she had seen, she had addressed right away, which consisted of room-service hours and not enough towels in the bathroom.

Brie had on a white pencil skirt with a lilac-colored sleeveless blouse and decided to visit the worksite to see how it was going after sending the emails. She hadn't been there in a while, and she needed to get out the office for a few minutes. Leaving her cell phone, she walked next door, loving the fresh lake breeze that was blowing over the area. She climbed up the stairs to the third floor and saw Xander and Doug bent over a table; the latter pointing to something on the blueprints.

"Hi, fellas," she greeted, approaching them.

"I really wish you'd have on a hard hat when you come in here," Xander said as he went to get one for her. Brie mouthed an apology to Doug, and he shrugged it away just as Xander handed her the protective piece.

"I just came over to check on things," she stated to Xander with a hand on her hip.

"It's going good. We're getting ready to construct the steel beams to the building."

"And who does that?" she wondered.

"Typically, the iron worker."

"Well, that makes sense." She giggled, and Xander inwardly smiled while taking in her outfit.

"Hey Brie, did you—" Xander's question was cut off when he heard some of his men yelling from above and felt the floor rattle. Instinct took over and he ran to Brie, pushing her out the way before a big light fixture crashed from the ceiling to the space where she had been standing. It landed on the table and caused it to tip over.

Xander had covered Brie's body with his, and she was trembling under him. Her hands were gripping his shirt in a tight grasp, and her breath was coming out in rapid pants. Xander looked down at her; his eyes scanning over her body to make sure she wasn't injured.

"Are you all right?" Xander inquired, breathing heavily. She nodded, her eyes staring intensely into his. When Xander tackled her, she didn't know what was happening until it was over. The workers rushed over to them and the fallen fixture. Xander bounced up on his feet and helped Brie stand up. Her body was still shaking, and she held onto his hand while she brushed the dirt from her clothes.

"Are you all right, Miss. Calhoun?" Doug asked in a worried voice.

"Yes, thank you," she whispered. She really was OK. It was just the severity of the situation that made her aware that this was a dangerous occupation. Brie heard Doug tell Xander he was going to find out what happened and ran upstairs.

"Are you good, Xander?" Brie asked, her eyes quickly checking out his body to make certain he was fine.

"Yeah, let's get you—" He paused when he saw blood on her skirt. She looked down and saw it as well. Slightly lifting her skirt, she saw a long cut on her outer left thigh.

"Oh, crap," she muttered, feeling the pain of the cut once she spotted it. Xander picked her up and headed for the entrance.

"Xander! What are you doing?" she asked in a high-pitched voice, wrapping her arm around his warm neck. She felt his strong arm under her knees and the solid support at her back and knew he wouldn't let her fall.

"Taking you back to the hotel so I can take you to the hospital," he explained. Marshall pulled up in the company truck with lunch and saw Xander walking out with Brie in his arms. With a scowl, he went to the site to find out what the hell happened.

"Xander, I can walk. You don't have to take me to the hospital," Brie told him as he carried her through the lobby. Luckily, Elmo wasn't around so she wouldn't have to explain what transpired. An elevator was waiting in the lobby, and he got on, hitting the button for the correct floor.

"You don't want to track in blood and scare your patrons, do you?"

Brie hadn't thought of that. She didn't want to alarm anyone, and she was glad he mentioned it. Ms. Darla wasn't at her desk since it was her day off, and Xander went inside her clean office, placing her on the couch.

"You have to go to the hospital, Brie, for insurance purposes," Xander explained, standing in front of her.

"Normally, I would agree, but it's a simple scratch. I don't want to sit in the emergency room for hours just for them to slap on antiseptic and a bandage. I'm waiving away medical treatment, and I'll sign any forms you need me to for your company. There's a first-aid kit in the restroom cabinet." Brie informed him, taking off her heels.

He hesitated, knowing she should go because she got hurt on company grounds, but she was an adult, and he couldn't force her to go. It really was a simple injury and could be tended to in less than ten minutes. Xander got the kit, noticing the bathroom was small, but it served its purpose. Xander got down on his haunches and opened the big box as she shimmied the skirt up past the cut.

"This is a big first-aid box," he noted to keep his mind focused on the task at hand. Her perfume had snuck up on him, and he tried to keep his mind from thinking sexual thoughts, especially since her thighs had become more exposed. Her soft, nutmeg-toned skin was causing his senses to go on overload, and he cleared his throat.

"I keep it handy for everyone, and they're stationed all over the hotel. Never know when it might be needed." She interrupted his wayward thoughts as he was putting on plastic gloves.

"Like now?"

Brie chuckled at that. "Like now," she agreed. "Xander, I can do this. Really." This was an intimate setting, and she didn't know how she'd react once his hands touched her, and she didn't want to find out either.

"This cut is under the thigh, Brie. At least let me do it the first time so you'll know it's properly cleaned and dressed." He reasoned, and she pouted.

He's gotta stop being so sensible all the time, she said to herself.

"But promise me you'll go to the hospital if it gets worse."

"I will."

"No, say it, Brie." Xander was insistent with his words, and she gazed into his worrying eyes, knowing he needed to hear the words.

115

"I promise I'll go to the hospital if it gets worse," Brie affirmed, and he nodded.

Xander grabbed a pillow from the couch and placed it on the glass table in front of the sofa. Gently raising her injured leg, he placed it on the cushion and reached for the mending supplies. Brie watched as he poured rubbing alcohol on a gauze and pressed it against the wound. Brie gasped and clutched his wrist at the burning pain.

"I'm sorry, Brie."

"No, it's fine. Thank you for pushing me out the way, Xander," she said in a soft voice, looking as he tended to her. Xander was attentive as he applied both alcohol and peroxide to the cut. He probably didn't have to use both liquids, but he realized that he wanted to keep his hands on her as long as possible and doing so provided him an excuse.

As he was waiting on the peroxide to do its job, Xander looked at Brie again and it was something different that time. Gratitude? Of course. Appreciation and wanting? Lust? Brie mentally shook her head at that last part. No. It couldn't be. They were friends, and he was married.

Yeah, keep telling yourself y'all are just friends, her

conscious hissed.

"You're welcome," he responded after being quiet for a few minutes.

Was he just looking at my lips? "How did you know what was happening?" she inquired, and he shrugged.

"Instinct. I felt the vibration, and my construction mind registered that something had fallen."

"I see your football reflexes are still sharp," Brie mentioned, and he grinned, causing those adorable smile lines to appear next to his eyes.

"Thanks for noticing." Xander reached for a bandage, and he wrapped his hands around her thigh as he applied two big bindings. As soon as his gloved palms curled around her flesh, she was lost. Although he had on protective wear, Brie felt the heat from his hands, and dammit… she liked it.

It caused wonderful surges to cascade up and down both legs, even though only one was being cared for. Her body betrayed her, and there was nothing Brie could do about it. Her nipples became hard and constrained against her blouse. Her skin felt hot like her blood vessels had increased in size.

Brie shuddered and licked her lips. "Xander…" She

placed her hand on his arm, and he glanced up from cleaning the dry blood. He'd have to be blind not to see Brie was aroused. From her breathless pants to her visible nipples, she was beyond hot and bothered from his simple touch, and he was surprised, amazed, and flattered at the same time.

Hell, he was feeling all the same emotions with horny being at the top of the list. His hand moved to her knee, and she flicked her tongue over her glossy bottom lip. "Brie…" The elevator doors pinged, and they heard voices heading toward the office.

Brie quickly stood up and headed for the bathroom, mumbling something about changing clothes. Marshall and Doug walked into the room as Xander was cleaning up. He was slow at the task so he could calm down and give time for his erection to go away. Xander could literally smell Brie's aroused scent, and it damn near had him panting like a dog in heat.

"Doug caught me up with what happened. Is Brie well?" Marshall asked his business partner.

"Yes, she just has a scrape. Did you figure out what happened?" Xander questioned Doug.

"The wiring holding the fixture was rusted and worn. It couldn't support the weight of the light anymore I'm assuming. The crew is going through and removing all the fixtures now." Xander nodded, reaching over to toss the garbage in the small waste basket near the sofa.

"Was anyone else hurt?"

Doug shook his head at the question, and Marshall glanced at the closed bathroom door. "Is Brie really OK?"

"Yeah, I think she was shaken up, but she's fine."

"Good thing you were there, bro."

Xander stood up when he felt he had cooled down enough to function and focus on the conversation. What happened between him and Brie... he was going to revisit with her and get some clarity. Brie stepped out the washroom wearing tan trousers and a white shirt.

"Hi, guys. No one else got injured, did they?" She didn't dare look at Xander after what happened. Especially since her thighs still sizzled from his hands.

"No, Ms. Calhoun."

"Good. I'll just stay from over there for a while."

"I just got back from getting lunch if you care to join us."

119

"Thank you, Marshall, but I have to get back to my work." They spoke for a few more minutes, then all three men left. Xander turned back to look at Brie; confusion and understanding in their eyes.

****

Later that night, after Xander finished eating a tuna sandwich and soup that Starr had made, he went upstairs to shower. The married couple had minimal conversation when he got home. Starr had stumbled into the house a few minutes after he got there, and she had told him she spent the day shopping, even though she didn't have any bags with her.

Xander stripped naked and stepped into the glass, cube-shaped shower. He had both water heads going, and he was enjoying the hot liquid. No matter how hard he tried, he couldn't get today out his mind. It was nothing to push Brie from harm's way. He remembered how small and perfect her body felt under him. But what happened in her office had left him speechless.

Xander knew he wouldn't have kissed her; not that he didn't want to but because he wasn't going to shame his marriage vows. He probably left his hand on her longer than necessary, but he was hypnotized after that look she gave him when she called his name. Her voice sounded raspy yet lustful at the same time. Hell, he wanted to do more than touch her, which is why he laid a hand on her knee. He saw the wanting and desire in her eyes and peeped her nipples standing at attention, and they were begging for him to lick and suck on them.

He closed a soapy hand around his hard dick and thought about Brie as he jerked off. Her smiling face, her sense of humor, her great legs, and her satin-smooth skin floated around in his mind as his hand was moving up and down in a slow movement. Xander imagined she had big, dark nipples and rested his head against the wet tile, and an intense orgasm ripped through him; a thick, big load shooting from his aching penis.

"Shit!" He roared under the sound of the water. He couldn't be a married man and thinking about another woman as he rubbed one out. He chalked it up to the several months without sex as the reason why he masturbated to thoughts of Brie.

OK, you got it out of your system. Not happening again,

he echoed to himself. Xander's dick bounced as he pictured how her juicy, bubbly ass formed against the skirt she was wearing earlier. "One more time, and that's it," he mumbled as he stroked his nine-inch cock; Brie once again the center of his attention.

At home, Brie sat on her bed after taking a long shower. She had a towel wrapped around her body and had just applied her favorite flower-scented lotion. Her mind was still juggling the details of what went down with Xander. One thing was for sure: her body was still craving his touch. She was so glad that Marshall and Doug had shown up when they did. She didn't trust herself to not have leaned forward and tried to kiss Xander.

That bothered her on a lot of levels because she didn't mess with married men, and she knew Xander was an honorable guy. But she wanted to… oh, God, how she wanted to feel his lips and savor his tongue! If she had responded like that from just a touch, she could only imagine how it would've been if they had proceeded.

Seeing as though it would never happen, it might not do her any good to think about it. But tell that to her traitorous body. She was still wet, still tender between her legs. She considered bringing out her vibrator, which she hadn't used in over a year. Her cell phone rang, and she was glad for the distraction away from her erotic, sexual thoughts.

"Hi, Brie, it's Natalie."

"Hey, girl. How are you?" Brie asked with a smile, putting Natalie on speaker phone as she slipped on a white sleep shirt.

"I'm good. I didn't mean to call you so late," Natalie expressed as Brie got in the bed and turned on the TV.

"9:30 isn't late. What's up?"

"I wanted to invite you to our annual 4th of July party. It's at our lake house in Kankakee."

"For real?"

"Yeah, we have a big swimming pool, but the house is a few yards from the lake. We're going to have tons of food, drinks, and games."

"It sounds like it'll be fun."

"It will be. You should come if you're not working."

"That's a weekend I'm off," Brie assured her.

"Good. You have two weeks to find a cute swimsuit." Natalie informed her, and Brie giggled.

"Can I bring a friend?"

"Absolutely; the more the merrier." Brie decided to ask Qyle, who would likely go, and she could act as a buffer.

"We'll be there. I'll bring something."

"You don't have to," Natalie insisted, taking a sip of juice.

"No, it's fine, I'll bring something."

"Great! I'll text you the address." They disconnected minutes later, and Brie turned off the bedside lamp to watch TV. She was laying on top of her comforter with the air conditioner on at a comfortable level. Huffing out a deep breath, Brie got up and went to her closet and pulled out her silver vibrator. Inserting new batteries, she climbed back in bed and slid the bullet inside her damp vagina. It only took a few seconds for her to have a spine-tingling release; Xander's name slipping past her lips.

Chapter 8

Qyle pulled up at the lake house and saw several cars parked on a dirt road. "Is this it?" she asked as Brie double checked the address and nodded. They got out of the convertible and grabbed the items from the backseat. Brie had a tote bag with a swimsuit and a change of clothes and two foil pans of pineapple shrimp kabobs. Qyle picked up the case of beer and soda, and they followed the music of the Sugar Hill Gang to a backyard area where the party was in full effect.

There was a huge Bermuda L-shaped pool with an outside shower under a rubber mat. There were two cabanas, lounge chairs, and a concrete deck with a white marble ledge where people were sitting and eating. Three rectangle tables had been set with food and drinks were cooling in a big, portable freezer. There was a volleyball net in the shallow end of the pool, and a few people were playing. Other guests sat at square tables playing cards and board games.

"Damn! They party like this?" Qyle asked, and Brie chuckled.

Natalie spotted the new guests, and she went to greet them, and she was wearing a yellow and blue sarong. "Hi, girl."

"Hey, Natalie. This is my best friend, Qyle Montoya. Qyle, this is Natalie Thornton, Marshall's wife."

"Thanks for the invite," Qyle said as she shook Natalie's hand.

"You're welcome. Let me show you where you can put the goodies. You all didn't have to bring anything. We have plenty of food and drinks."

"We don't get down like that," Qyle replied, and the hostess smiled.

"Well, if you both want to swim, you can change in the cabana. If not, you can do whatever you want, and the fireworks start at nine." Natalie informed them after they dropped off the food and drink.

"You swimming?" Brie questioned Qyle, who shook her head.

"No, I'm good," she remarked, looking at the bikini-clad women. While Brie went to change, Starr was sitting on a lounge chair with her phone clutched in her hand. Today was the Mandingo yacht party, and she was waiting on Casey to text her when she got outside.

Starr had on a blue mini skirt with a matching

handkerchief top with large-framed sunglasses. Xander had asked if she wanted or needed anything, but she told him no. *It was a nice gathering,* Starr admitted. But she was ready to get on the yacht and have some fun. She had been thinking about the boat party all week, and she couldn't wait to see what the night held.

Xander was in the pool, laughing and enjoying the water games. A friendly game of water volleyball was going on, and the teams involved were having a good time. Two people had gotten out the cool water, and the game participants were hanging out until it started back up.

"Oh, hey, Ms. Calhoun," Doug said to Brie, who approached from behind Xander.

"Hi, guys! Need another player?"

"Sure. C'mon over." Xander turned around and damn near drooled on himself. Brie had changed into a two-piece, red-white-and-blue swimsuit that was held together by plastic clips. In his mind, Brie's body was covered in boils and spots just to keep him from picturing anything else.

But to see her flat tummy with her toned thighs and plush breasts crushed the notion he had. Now that Xander had an accurate picture, the ideas of scars and sores were now gone. Xander had on black swim trunks, and when he stood up, the water came to his stomach.

Ignoring the need to talk to her, another game got underway, and Xander tried to keep his eyes off Brie's bouncing tits whenever she jumped to hit the ball. Starr looked down at her phone when it went off and saw Casey's message: *Pulling up now*. She'd wait three minutes then make an excuse to leave.

Xander went over to the pool's edge and rested his arms against it, looking at his wife. "Starr, c'mon and join the game. It's fun."

"No, I'm good," she said quickly, glancing at her cell.

"Are you just going to sit there and not socialize with anyone?" Xander prodded, and she adjusted her sunglasses.

"I'm fine right here."

"You look hot. Maybe you should cool off." Xander had said it as a joke as he splashed some water her way and a few drops landed on her legs.

"Xander! Look what you did? I'm soaked!" Starr's raised voice caused people to look their way with interest. She grabbed her purse and left the deck. Xander hopped out the pool and stormed into the house in anger.

Brie looked at the scene and was left speechless. She thought that Starr had overreacted. It was only water, not fire, and it only got on her legs. She felt bad for Xander, knowing Starr had embarrassed him. The game ended, and she swam a few laps before getting out. Brie showered and changed her clothes in the cabana that consisted of white shorts and a peach-colored halter top.

She made herself a plate and sat at a table with a woman who had an eight-month-old baby. An hour later, she had gotten up from a spades game and went to go look at the lake from the deck. She spotted Xander sitting on the sand with his arms resting on his raised knees. Brie went to the cooler and grabbed some beverages before taking the wooden steps down to the beach.

"I didn't know if you were thirsty, so I brought a few options," she offered, holding out a beer, water, and Pepsi.

Xander glanced at her and reached for the alcoholic beverage. "Thank you." He popped the top and drank half of the bottle.

"Do you want some company?" she asked him after he didn't say anything for a minute.

"Sure." She sat next to him and dug her toes into the cool sand. Some people were jet skiing and playing in the water a few yards away. The unopened drinks sat next to her, and Brie looked at his profile, not knowing what to say. This was a party, and she wanted him to get back in his good mood.

Brie nudged him with her shoulder and stretched her legs out. "What do you call a sleeping bull?"

Xander looked at her with weary eyes, then back at the calm water. "I don't know."

"A bulldozer."

Xander's mouth twitched to keep from grinning, and she smiled with sparkling eyes.

"Go on and laugh. You know you wanna."

Xander chuckled and shook his head. "That was so corny, Brie."

"But you laughed," she insisted, and he smiled at that.

"Do you want to talk about it?"

He sighed and drank some more beer. "Not particularly."

"Xander, it's the 4th of July. You don't want to spend your time down here brooding. I'm sure Starr will want to talk about it when you get home and apologize."

Xander regarded her, his hands still clutching the bottle. "You think she should apologize?"

"Oh, without a doubt. She caused a scene for no reason and embarrassed you."

He didn't know what to say. Brie was a spectator and thought Starr was wrong for what she did. Xander frowned at the thought that Brie continued to amaze him at every turn.

"How's your leg?"

"It's better now. Thanks for asking."

"Brie!" They turned around and saw Qyle running toward her in a hurry. "Hey, the Extreme Striker people called, and I have to fly back to Atlanta. Can you get a ride home?" her friend asked as she was talking to her and reading a text message at the same time.

"Yeah, sure. Let me know what happens." Qyle nodded and headed for her car.

"What's up with Extreme Striker?" Xander wondered, giving her his attention.

"Qyle is trying to negotiate a deal for one of her clients."

He finished the drink and placed it next to him.

"She must get a lot of tickets to sporting events." Brie nodded, sifting sand through her fingers.

"I'll give you a ride home," he told her after a few minutes, and her heart rate increased at that.

"What?" She squeaked out, her throat suddenly dry.

"I said I'll take you home. And don't try to talk me out of it."

"OK, sheesh." He had an amused look on his face and nudged her back with his shoulder. Xander decided Brie was right. It was a nice party going on, and he wasn't going to let his wife ruin his good time.

"C'mon, let's go back upstairs." Xander helped her up, and they joined the festivities. When nightfall arrived, the fireworks show started, and the bursts of colors danced off the calm surface of the water. Some people watched from the deck and others went down to the lake to get a better view.

Brie was leaning against the ledge, enjoying the sights, and Xander stood by the pool; his eyes locked on Brie. He was thankful she had come down and talked with him. She had gotten him out his funky mood, and he ended up having a good time. He wished Starr was like Brie but couldn't compare cantaloupes to grapefruit. Starr was his wife, and he'd continue to honor that.

****

Starr, on the other hand, wasn't thinking about the scene she had caused at the BBQ. She was on a nice ass yacht having the best night ever. She had just passed the blunt to someone else, and she sauntered toward a black guy who was sitting at the back of the motor boat yacht with his dick hanging out. It was anchored in Lake Michigan, but it was far away where they wouldn't be interrupted by the other boaters in the area. Casey had introduced Starr as soon as they boarded, but she had forgotten names and licked her lips when she saw a tall African man grab Casey by the shoulders and pushed her to her knees in front of him.

Including her and Casey, there were two other women on board and a total of seven guys. Starr went over to the stranger, lifted her skirt and exhaled in pleasure as he slid inside her ass. The guy ran his hands up her breasts and squeezed hard as Starr was fucking him raw. Another woman came over to them, and she bent her head to kiss Starr on her mouth; her skin fizzing with anticipation when three other men walked over to the threesome and undid their pants.

****

Xander pulled up in front of Brie's townhouse in the Kenwood area and took notice of the neighborhood. It seemed like a quiet area, and there were a lot of nice-looking residences.

"Would you like to come in for a few minutes?" Brie asked when he turned off his SUV.

"Actually, yes, I need to use your restroom." Brie chuckled, and they exited the car. Walking into the house, they were hit with a brush of cold air, and it felt good to Xander.

"The bathroom is right there." She pointed out the door down the hall. She took her shoes off and placed her tote bag on the kitchen floor after turning the TV on and plugging in her cell phone.

Xander came out, drying his hands on a paper towel and looked around her place. "This is nice," he mentioned, looking at the color-coordinated furniture and accessories.

"Thanks. Do you want something to drink?"

"No, I'm good. Can I sit down?" She nodded, and he sat

on the slate-color, cushioned chair, and she sat on the sofa with her legs folded Indian style.

"How long will it take you to get home?" she inquired, flipping through the channels and settled on *The Ghostbusters*.

"Trying to get rid of me?" He returned with a smirk and she smiled.

"Of course not. I know people are driving, and they've been drinking. Just want to make sure you're safe."

Xander's heart warmed at that. "I'll be fine. I'm going to jump on Lake Shore Drive and take the 294 to Lombard."

She nodded, peeking at the clock on the VCR that showed 11:45 p.m. "Marshall and Natalie sure know how to throw a good party."

"Yeah, they're always hosting get-togethers and game nights."

"That sounds fun."

"We actually need some competition. Marshall and I are reigning spades champs," Xander bragged, and she beamed at that.

"Is that right? Maybe you need to play some real spades players."

135

"Are you offering?"

Brie shrugged. "I haven't played in a minute."

"It's cool. I'll be gentle." She rolled her eyes with amusement and settled back on the couch.

"Are you still active with your fraternity?"

"No, but I donate to causes and volunteer at some events. I just gave a thousand dollars to the Alpha scholarship program to give to the young man who is selected."

"That was nice of you." He shrugged; Brie noticing he wasn't comfortable with being praised. They looked at the movie, watching as Slimmer attacked Dr. Venkman.

"Have you heard from your friend?"

"Qyle? No, not yet. She'll text sooner or later."

"How did you two meet, by the way?" Xander pondered, stretching his legs out. Brie told him the story, and he hung onto her every word.

"And you two have been friends since?"

"Yes. She's a bit overprotective ever since Walter, but I've told her to lighten up."

"Who's that?"

"My ex-boyfriend," she answered softly.

"Why did you two break up?"

"Kind of a personal question, don't you think?" She shot back, and he shifted in the chair.

"It is. Sorry. You don't have to answer." She stared at him, rearranging her legs under her.

"I broke up with him because he cheated on me," she told him in a low voice.

"I'm sorry to hear that. How long did you date?"

"About three years. Now we have the kind of relationship where he asks me where to take his dates and what to wear to impress them… it's weird."

"Does he want to get back together?" Brie didn't know why she was talking to Xander about these things, but it felt peaceful. She hadn't heard from Walter in a while and hadn't even thought about him.

"No. But if he does, it's not going to happen."

"That's good. You have your principles." Something inside Xander was glad to hear that. He almost jumped for joy, but he played it cool. He was also happy to hear that she wouldn't subject herself to that type of toxic relationship again.

"I just don't understand why people cheat if they're supposed to be in a committed relationship. If you want to sleep around, that's fine, but don't be attached to someone and cheat on them." Xander's heart slammed in his chest at what she said. He had the same thought process, and something in his mind told him that she'd be a loyal and honest woman in a relationship.

"Yeah—" Xander cleared his throat, "Yeah, I feel the same way."

"The rules are different for married people though." She pointed out.

"Well, of course. They made a commitment before God with vows. If infidelity is involved, that presents a problem."

Brie licked her lips before asking her next question. "Have you ever been tempted while married?"

Yes, by you! his conscience screamed. It was only fair that she asked him a personal question since he had asked one.

"When I was playing ball and on the road travelling, there would be some women who would sneak into some hotel rooms; mine included. They thought if they wore scantily-clad outfits or nothing at all, I'd be all over them." Xander recalled

138

the numerous times he had to get security to escort women out his room in various cities the team played in.

"What did you do?"

"I asked them to leave or had security get rid of them." Brie let out a deep breath at his answer; not realizing she'd been holding it. She always knew he was an admirable man.

"Well, you can't blame them for trying. You are a nice guy."

"I don't think nice was on their minds when they snuck into my room." Brie laughed, and their eyes met again in silent exchange. Her phone pinged, and she got up to check her message. She grinned at the text and replied.

"That was Qyle; everything went good with the drink people. They signed her client."

"That's good. Tell her congratulations. Is she flying back now?"

"No, she's going to stay the night. Have you ever been to Atlanta?" she asked when she sat back down on the couch.

"A few times. It's nice there. You?"

"No, haven't had the chance yet. The last place I visited was Vegas." They continued their conversation about the places they'd been to and wanted to go, their favorite movies, sports teams, and a few teachers they liked and disliked from school.

Brie looked at the clock and saw that it was after two a.m. "Oh, wow! We've been talking for hours," Brie exclaimed, yawning.

"I hadn't noticed." It had been too much fun talking to her about different things. He couldn't remember the last time he and Starr had stayed up so late together to talk.

"Are you OK driving home? Do you need me to make you some coffee to keep you up?" she asked as she walked him to the front door.

"I'm good, Brie."

"Can you text me and let me know you made it home safely?" she requested of him, leaning against the wall.

Xander grinned at that. "Yes, ma'am." They faced each other, and that moment was upon them again. That silent, easy, unspoken moment. It wasn't as intense as the one from her office, but it was still just as evident. A lot was said with their eyes, but they didn't speak on it.

"Good night, Brie."

"Good night, Xander." He brushed past her in a whisper, their bodies passing one another in a quiet touch. Brie locked the door behind him and threw her head back against it, closing her eyes. *You are lost, girl.*

It didn't bother Xander that Starr wasn't home when he walked in forty-five minutes later. He was on such a high from being near Brie and talking to her. He sent her a quick text like she asked of him, and she replied with a smiley face. Inside the bedroom, Xander pulled his clothes off and took a shower. This was beginning to be his favorite time because he loved taking long showers, and he could let his mind wander toward Brie. Xander moaned with pleasure as he stroked himself; this time, flashes of Brie's bikini-clad body drifted in his head.

He had exploded three times, and that was enough to tire him out for the night. The next afternoon, Starr walked downstairs and saw her husband finishing his oatmeal and fruit. It was after four in the morning when she got in, which was good because he had been asleep, and she didn't want to explain herself.

"Good afternoon," she greeted in a timid voice, wearing a nightgown. Xander got up from the table, placed his dishes in the sink, and went downstairs to the basement without saying a word. *This is not good*, Starr thought to herself.

Chapter 9

It was two weeks later, and clear progress could be seen with the construction. Metal beams were being erected with bolts and welding, then the frame was being secured with the proper materials. Besides casual passing, Brie and Xander didn't have the opportunity to talk. He was in the office, catching up on some paperwork with Marshall. It was a gloomy day with dark clouds, and rain threatened to fall at any moment.

Marshall walked in, attaching his phone on his belt clip after sending a text message. "I'm getting ready to file the paperwork for the Naperville job. Do you have the purchase invoices?" Xander nodded as he stood up, went to the file cabinet, and got the folder that Marshall requested.

"Thanks. What are your plans for the weekend?"

"I don't know. What's up?"

"Just asking. I think Natalie and I will just chill." Xander nodded, sitting back in the chair as he played with his pen.

"How are things with you and Starr?"

"The same," Xander answered with a shrug, and Marshall shook his head at that.

"I don't even know what I'd do in your situation." Xander didn't know how to respond. To say the dynamics of his marriage had changed was an understatement. It wasn't a sudden change either. Like he told his father, it had been happening for months. It wasn't just her behavior. He and Starr didn't talk anymore, nor did they have date nights. They didn't laugh together anymore and didn't have fun.

Hell, it felt like they weren't even a couple. His parents had been married for fifty-four years, and Xander wanted that. He wanted someone to grow old with. To be up in his years and be content, satisfied, and peaceful with his wife. He genuinely didn't see that with Starr anymore. It had nothing to do with his confusing and growing fondness for Brie. He and Starr were having problems way before then.

Starr had walked out the elevator and waved to the receptionist as she headed toward her husband's office. She wanted to see if he was available for lunch and hoped he wouldn't turn her down. The office door was ajar, and she paused in the hallway and overheard Xander's conversation with Marshall. Starr knew she shouldn't be listening, but she'd get a sense of Xander's feelings from hearing him talk to his best friend.

"I don't know either. It's only so much a man can take, you know?" Marshall agreed with that, shifting the file in his hands.

"Have you talked to Brie?"

Who the hell is that? Starr wondered to herself.

"No. I haven't had the chance; we've both been busy."

"Well, I hope things get better between you and Starr," Marshall mentioned, and Starr walked away before she heard that part. She wondered if Xander was cheating on her, and that stung worse than she thought. She had tears in her eyes as she left the building and made a point to have a talk with Xander as soon as he got home.

****

Hours later, Starr was sitting on the couch in the living room with the lights off. She had the radio on low, and her legs were curled under her. She knew she did her dirt and a lot of it was toward Xander. She had cheated on him with multiple people and lied to him. But to find out that Xander was having an affair… Starr admitted that hurt a lot. She knew she was being the biggest hypocrite in the world, but she didn't care. Starr heard Xander walk into the house, and she let out a deep breath. *Here goes nothing.*

Xander placed his keys on the kitchen counter and walked in to see Starr sitting in the dark. "Hey. What's going on?" he asked, turning on the lamp.

"Can you sit down? We need to talk," Starr said to him, and he sat on the ottoman across from her.

"What's up?"

"Who is Brie?"

"She's our client on the hotel job."

"Are you sleeping with her?"

"No, Starr. How do you know about her, and why are you asking me these questions?" Starr was taken aback; she had expected some hesitation or avoidance, but Xander answered right away.

"I came to the office earlier to see if you wanted to have lunch, and I overheard you and Marshall talking."

"You mean eavesdropping."

"Call it what you want, but I heard Marshall ask if you had talked to her." Xander cleared his throat and sighed deeply. *Is she really having this conversation right now?*

"So because you heard Marshall ask if I had spoken to Brie, that means I'm sleeping with her?" Starr licked her dry lips at his inquiry. She hadn't thought this out. It would make sense for them to be in contact with their clientele.

"There was a tone in your voice, Xander." She defended weakly.

"In case you haven't noticed, Starr, I haven't paid any other woman any attention since we've been together. And I find it funny that you're accusing me of cheating when you're the one whose coming in at crazy hours, hiding your cell phone, and acting secretly." He threw back at her with a raised voice.

"Xander, I want to repair our relationship. I don't like us like this." Starr informed him, moving to the edge of the couch.

"How do you plan to fix it? We don't talk. We don't go out. You're not fucking me, and you won't let me touch you," Xander said, looking at her. She was a year younger than him, but she looked older than that. Her eyes were tired, and her skin wasn't as clear as it used to be.

"I've been thinking about it; we should go see a marriage

counselor," she announced, watching his face for a reaction.

He wasn't expecting her to say that, and he was surprised that she suggested it. He wasn't one to air out his dirty laundry to strangers, but maybe this was what they needed. An objective third party could help them get their marriage back on track.

"Please consider it. I'll do everything, Xander. I'll look for a therapist, schedule the appointment, and everything. Please say you'll consider it."

Xander let out another deep breath, knowing he would say yes. He didn't want it to be known that he didn't try everything to save his marriage. "OK, Starr. You make the arrangements and let me know when to be there."

****

Taking advantage of a quiet day, Brie was sitting on the couch in her office, putting together a few employee evaluations for their annual review. In addition to meeting with the employees and their department supervisors, guest comments played a part in the assessment process. She was stapling paperwork for fourteen people when her cell phone rang and got excited when she saw who the caller was.

"Daddy!"

"Hey, honey."

"Why haven't you called before now?" she urged, settling back on the couch.

"Shoot, I been having too much fun." Brie laughed at that, folding her legs.

"How's the cruise going?"

"I should've retired a long time ago. I'm so relaxed and at peace," Theo replied to her.

"I'm glad to hear that. Where are you now?"

"We're heading to Greece," Theo answered, taking a sip of lemonade.

"Oh, that sounds wonderful! I know Tillie is enjoying herself."

"She is. And we keep meeting all these interesting people."

"Well, that's good too. You know how you like to talk to people. Don't forget to bring me some souvenirs."

"I already have some for you."

"Did you call to check up on things?"

"Nope." Brie smiled at that. "I trust your judgement. I just

149

called to check in with you and let you know I'm fine. I know how you get."

Theo grinned when he heard Brie giggle. "Thanks for checking in, Daddy."

The father and daughter talked for another half hour before she hung up. She was happy her dad was having fun on his cruise. After all his years of working, he certainly deserved this time off. A few minutes later, her cell phone went off again, and she answered the call.

"Hi, Natalie."

"Hey, Brie. Are you busy?"

"Always, but I can take a break. What's going on?"

"I have a few minutes in between classes, so I wanted to call and invite you to game night on Saturday." Brie inwardly smiled; remembering Xander's words about how she liked to throw parties.

"Will it be a lot of people like that 4th of July party?"

"Oh, no! That's a once a year thing. It's just four people, including you if you say yes."

Brie sighed and uncrossed her legs. She should go. Maybe it would keep her mind off Xander. She hadn't spoken to him since the party a few weeks ago, and it wasn't like she could just text or call him.

"Yeah. Sure, I'll come."

"Great! Bring a sweater just in case. We're going to be at the lake house, and I'm ordering Mexican food." Brie got excited for the upcoming plans. Games and adult conversations were always a good thing. *This could be just the thing to keep your mind off a certain married guy,* her inner voice reminded her, and she nodded at that.

****

Marshall and Xander were in the basement of the lake house playing a game of Mortal Kombat, which was part of their game-night ritual. They would play a few rounds of the video game to get in the winning state of mind. Both had on jeans, but Xander had on a white hoodie, and Marshall was wearing a beige, long-sleeved shirt. The card table had been set up on the patio, and a big fire brewed in the pit a few feet away. The food had been set up on the counter in the kitchen, and Natalie had just finished putting chips and salsa into wooden bowls.

"Who is Natalie's partner tonight?" Xander asked as the

Johnny Cage character he was playing with jumped to avoid one of Raiden's special moves.

"I don't know. Maybe one of her co-workers or someone from her book club. Either way, they're losing," Marshall stated, and Xander chuckled. He was glad he was here tonight. Even though Starr had kept her word and found a marriage counselor, nothing had changed between them. Their conversations were few and far in between, and when she left the house at two that afternoon, she didn't mention where she was headed.

When Xander left to head to the lake house, she hadn't returned home and wasn't answering her calls, and he honestly didn't care at this point. Xander decided to keep it real with himself and admitted that he missed Brie. He wondered what she was doing tonight, and if she was OK.

"Man! Stop cheating!" Marshall's words bought Xander out his reverie, and he grinned; neither man paying attention when the doorbell rang.

Brie was glad she had followed Natalie's advice and bought a sweater. She felt a chill in the air as she waited for the door to open, but it wasn't an uncomfortable one. She was wearing cuffed jeans, a purple shirt, and a white sweater that hung off one shoulder.

"Hey, Brie," Natalie greeted her with a hug, and she returned the gesture.

"Hey, girl. I bought sangria," she announced, holding up a big bottle.

"Cool, it'll go well with the food. Let me show you around before we start playing. The men are downstairs having their game-night ceremonial fun."

Brie laughed as Natalie showed her around the four-bedroom place. It was bigger than she expected, and she loved the spacious rooms with the big windows. Once they got to the oval-shaped kitchen, Natalie paused at the basement door while Brie looked over the yummy offering.

"Do you mind opening the wine? I'll go get the guys." Brie nodded, reaching out to grab a chip. Natalie bounced down the carpeted steps and stood next to Marshall's recliner chair.

"Who's winning?" Natalie asked, running her fingers over the back of his head.

"No one. We're just playing."

"My partner is here, so we can get the spades game going

after we eat." Xander went upstairs as Marshall pulled his wife to sit on him in the chair. He paused when he saw Brie pouring a glass of wine. His heart jumped when he saw her, and he was able to get an eyeful of her backside because her back was to him. Brie turned around and gasped when she saw Xander standing in the doorway.

"What are you doing here?" she asked more out of surprise, and his eyebrows went up.

"It's game night, Brie."

"But Natalie didn't say you'd be here. I thought it would be someone else. I didn't see your truck out front."

"I had to park two houses down," he simply answered, and she took a huge swallow of the fruity beverage.

Brie had not anticipated seeing him at all and wasn't expecting her body to respond when he was around. *How am I supposed to not think about him when he's always around?*

"Is it a problem that I'm here?" Xander waited for her to say something as he walked further into the kitchen to lean against the counter.

"No, it's fine." *Damn, he smells good!*

"Cool. How have you been?"

"I've been good. I heard from my dad this week. He's having a blast being away." Xander smiled at what she said, and she thought he looked so attractive.

"I know he is. He's probably going to make you go through all the vacation pictures."

"I wouldn't mind if he did." She let him know with a smile. "How's everything with you?"

Xander hesitated before answering. "Good. Um, Starr and I are going to see a marriage counselor next week." He didn't know why he was telling her but figured he could since they were friends and had talked about private matters before.

"Oh, that's good… it's healthy." He picked up a paper plate and walked toward the food.

"What are they doing downstairs?"

"Who knows? She's probably trying to get inside his head before we start playing cards." He had a good idea of what they were doing since they were a happy and devoted married couple. Brie stood behind him as he made his plate, taking in the span of his muscular back. They went to eat on the deck, and Xander took a sip of his beer.

"How far does the game usually go up to?" Brie asked,

eating a taco.

"The first team to seven hundred wins."

"I probably should tell you, I'm a good spades player." Xander nodded, not taking her seriously, and she smiled. The radio was on and "Strawberry Letter 23" was playing in the background.

"Marshall and I were asked to co-host the scholarship dinner in a few weeks."

"That's great! I thought you said you weren't going."

"I wasn't, but since they asked, I guess I am now."

"And they already know who's going to get the award?"

"Yes, it's going to three young men. One of them is so damn smart. He got offered full rides to Harvard, Morehouse, and NYU and got over six million dollars in grants and scholarships."

"That is amazing! So this is a pretty big deal?"

"To them it is. There's a dinner, dancing, a slideshow, and the awards presentation." Marshall and Natalie came upstairs soon after, and they started the game an hour later.

Turns out, Brie was a damn good spades player. She was ruthless and cutthroat, and Xander was so turned on by it. The current game was tied, and both teams had twelve books with one card still left to be played to see who would win the hand. Brie had laughed so hard at the two men. They talked big stuff at the beginning when they won the first three games, but when the women started to come back, they got quiet. It was after 9:30 p.m., but they were having too much fun to notice the time. Natalie had caught the glances between Xander and Brie and made a mental note to talk to Marshall about it later.

"I hope you got it," Xander said to his partner, eyeing his King of spades.

"I hope *you* got it," Marshall returned, and Brie chuckled.

"You two are sad. How about we all throw out at the same time?" Natalie suggested, and they all threw in their cards; the guys cursing and yelling when Brie laid out the big joker. They ended up playing and talking for another three hours, and Xander trailed Brie home to make sure she got there safely. He didn't go in this time but nodded at her from his vehicle before heading home.

****

Xander sat in the lobby of Dr. Tomas Gomez's office, waiting on Starr to show up for their first appointment. He had come over from the office after telling Marshall that he was taking the afternoon off. On the drive over, he thought about the upcoming meeting and hoped to God that this would work. He honestly didn't know what the next step would be if this didn't pan out. He had just finished texting Starr again when the marriage counselor opened his office door.

"Mr. Sterling? Come on in, please." Dr. Gomez asked his receptionist to inform him when Starr arrived, and she acknowledged the request. It was a spacious office with wide windows that faced Grant Park. It was a tidy room that had a bookcase that held several books with wooden and metal art pieces placed across the top ledge. Colorful pieces of Mexican art graced the wall, and there was a tall, bushy plant in a corner. The therapist was an older Hispanic male with a friendly demure, and his long hair was in a ponytail that hung down his back and was speckled with gray hair.

"Would you like something to drink, Mr. Sterling?"

"No, I'm fine. Thank you."

"While we're waiting on Mrs. Sterling, do you mind if we talk?"

Xander nodded. "Sure. I don't have anything to hide."

Dr. Gomez uncapped his pen and opened a black, leather-bound ledger. "Obviously, you're here because of some discontentment in your marriage, but what do you hope these sessions will accomplish?" the doctor asked Xander, who shifted in his seat.

"You talked to my wife when she made the appointment. What did she tell you?"

"In my pre-interview, when I asked, I was told that you two had drifted apart, and there was a lot of tension in the marriage."

"Did she tell you why we're growing apart?"

"No, she didn't go into specifics." *Of course, she didn't,* Xander scoffed.

"How long have you been married?"

"Six years."

"When did you first start to notice a change?" Xander continued to answer Dr. Gomez's questions and when forty-five minutes had passed, Starr hadn't called or shown up. His hands were fisted in anger, and Dr. Gomez noticed the body language.

"Have you heard from your wife? You can try calling.

Maybe she got caught in traffic."

Xander called Starr again, and when it went to voicemail, he shook his head in disappointment. "I should've known she wouldn't go through with this. Don't worry, you can send the bill for this session," Xander uttered before storming out the office.

Hours later as Xander was waiting on Starr to get home, she was at Casey's house doing what she did best. Casey's current boyfriend had come over, and he had brought a friend. At first, he wasn't interested in Starr and was there just to get high from the cocaine Casey had. But after they had been drinking and snorting for over an hour, he had followed her to the spare bedroom, and she gave him a blow job. When she ended up in bed with him, Starr didn't think twice about the counseling appointment she missed. She was getting what she wanted and didn't care about anything else.

****

After the meeting with the counselor, he had waited up for Starr until one in the morning. When she got there, she didn't say anything to him; she just went to the bathroom and took a shower. At that moment, Xander moved his things into a spare bedroom. That was a week ago, and they had moved about the house like they were strangers. Starr tried to talk to him, she made him meals, rented videos, yet nothing worked. Dr. Gomez sent an invoice for three hundred dollars, and Xander gave it to Starr for her to pay it. He also did what his father suggested and took her off his personal bank account. He knew about her separate account and figured she could use that for whatever she needed. Xander had reached the end of his rope with her. He would talk to Starr eventually, but right now, he had nothing to say.

On a Thursday morning, at the construction site, Marshall gave a purchase order to Xander so he could go pick up the supplies they needed. Next door, at the hotel, Brie took an aspirin and rubbed her temples. She had been dealing with a difficult guest all morning, and she had a headache.

First, it took too long for check in, then she didn't like the comforter in the room. She complained about the wooden floor in the second room, and she didn't like where the bathroom was placed in the third room. The woman was finally satisfied with the fifth room she was shown, and Brie was glad because she was about to show her the roof next.

She walked out the hotel and to the side near the valet parking area to clear her head. She sat on a wooden bench and let out a deep breath as she closed her eyes. It wasn't even noon yet, and she felt drained. She appreciated the breeze that was coming from the lake and felt like she could sit on the bench all day.

"Brie? Are you OK?" Xander had seen her walk out the building when he was heading toward the company truck and followed her out of curiosity.

"Hey, Xander. Yes, I'm fine. Just been dealing with an irate guest for over an hour."

"It was that bad you had to step outside?" he asked in a deep breath, and she nodded slowly.

"Hey, listen, I'm getting ready to drive out to our supplier to pick up some things. You want to come with me?" Xander inquired, and she looked at him with surprise.

"Really?"

"Yes. You can keep me company, and it'll get you away from here for a while." Xander did make a good point, and it might do her some good to get away. Aside from the displeased customer, everything was going well, and Elmo could handle things while she was away.

"Sure, let me go change."

"I'll meet you at the truck."

Minutes later, she had let herself into the pickup truck, wearing red shorts and a white Chicago Bulls tank top. *She would wear tiny shorts*, he stated to himself. Xander headed towards Lake Shore Drive to jump on I-55. Traffic was mildly congested on the streets, so it took a few minutes before he was heading away from the city.

"Where do you go to get the supplies?"

"Beecher's. It's in Joliet."

"All the way out there?" He nodded as he merged with the traffic to get on the expressway. Brie watched as Xander maneuvered the steering wheel; the muscles in his arms flexing and were toned. "Mr. Telephone Man" came on the radio, and she started singing along. Xander smiled as he settled back in the seat, using one hand to drive.

"Is this your jam?"

"It's bringing back some memories," she stated, looking out the window. Dark clouds were forming in the direction they were heading, but that didn't stop Xander from going to get the materials.

"I would ask how the renovations are going, but I can see progress for myself."

"It's coming along. We found out the pipes busted at the place where the scholarship dinner was supposed to be held and it flooded. It's going to take weeks to pull the carpet and repair everything. Marshall suggested using one of the banquet halls at the hotel, so someone from the committee might be giving you a call." Xander notified her, and she was pleased at the news.

"Oh, I wasn't aware. I'll have to thank him for the recommendation."

"I believe they're still fishing around for spots, but I wanted to give you a heads up." Brie knew that one of the rooms had been reserved, and the other was free as of that morning, so if they called, Dynasty Towers could accommodate the event. It was almost an hour later when they pulled up to the busy warehouse. Brie went to use the ladies' room while Xander shopped and had the merchandise loaded onto the truck.

Twenty minutes later, they left and stopped at a crowded

fast food place to grab lunch. After some debate, Brie had bought food for them, and they ate outside at one of the plastic tables.

"I always stop here when I come this way, and they have good food. You should've gotten their onion rings; they're famous," he said as he drank his soda.

"Are they? Can I have a few?"

"Uh huh." She smiled at that and took a bite of her Italian beef. Xander put a few of them on a napkin and pushed them her way.

"Thank you."

"You're welcome." He watched as she ate one, and she nodded at the taste. Xander ate his food at a fast pace, and soon it was gone, and she stared at him with raised eyebrows.

"Hungry?"

"Actually, I was." They were back on the road after eating, and Brie was glad she had decided to go with him. It was relaxed being in the car with him, and the conversations wasn't forced between them. He was humming "Bernadette" by The Four Tops, and rain began to fall.

"I like this truck. I like sitting up high like this. I can see over the cars."

"Maybe you should get one of these the next time you go car shopping," Xander suggested as the rain came down harder. He slowed it down as the wipers were going full speed. The traffic slowed down as well, and it turned into a crawl.

"Can you see, Xander?" she asked, looking at him.

"Not really." They hadn't reached Bolingbrook yet before he drove on the shoulder and turned on the hazard lights. It was literally coming down in buckets, and he turned the wipers off since there was no point in using them right now. He was glad he had put the cover over the tail of the truck so the purchases wouldn't get wet.

"This is crazy. I didn't know it was supposed to rain like this," she mentioned, looking at the slow traffic, and a few other cars pulled over to the side as well.

"Me either. Once it lets up, I'll get back on the road." Brie nodded and became mildly nervous. This was some fierce rain, and she understood why he pulled over, but she didn't expect to be in close quarters this long with him. *Just keep it cool. The rain shouldn't last too long*, she kept repeating to herself.

Xander glanced at Brie and felt her apprehension. He also expected it to be a turnaround trip, but this damn rain was not making it possible. Her scent was driving him crazy, and he started to go over football stats in his head to distract him.

"You good?" he asked, and she nodded. Up until now, they could talk at any time during the drive. But now, she had no words, and she wish she knew what to say.

"I have an idea. Let's play twenty questions until the rain stops."

"What?" he repeated himself, and she let out a lopsided grin.

"Are you serious?"

"Anything is better than sitting here not talking."

"Are we not talking, Xander?"

"We're not, *not* talking," he said, and she exhaled.

"Is there a no zone for the questions?"

"We'll play it by ear." *Fine, why not? Seems harmless enough.*

"I'll go first. Do you want kids?" Brie kicked it off, undid her seat belt, and faced him.

"Yes. Do you?"

She nodded. "How many boyfriends have you had?"

"Including Walter, only four and two were serious. How many girlfriends have you had?"

"Nine, with Starr." She seemed surprised, and he shrugged.

"Sowing your wild oats, huh?"

"That's not a bad number, and that counts as a question."

"Oh, crap!" Xander chuckled at that.

"Are you happy, Brie?"

"Yes," she answered without hesitation. "I'm content. Are you happy, Xander?"

He scratched his chin and looked out the window. Brie watched as many emotions showed on his face, and she took note that it took him a long time to answer. Was it not a simple question?

"I'm happy as far as my career, but with my marriage, no." She looked at him as he watched her. Xander kept eye contact with her, and her heart wept at his dejected tone.

"I'm sorry, Xander. I didn't mean to—"

"It's OK. When you do get married, do you want a big wedding?"

"Nah. Just something small with a few friends and family. Was your wedding big?"

"Yep. It was a lavish party, and I didn't know half the people, but that's what Starr wanted."

"And you aim to please?"

"'A happy wife is a happy life.'" He quoted the old saying, and she gave a brief nod. Brie bit her bottom lip and noticed that the rain hadn't let up yet.

"Are you attracted to me, Brie?" Xander asked softly, his thumbs resting on the steering wheel. She turned her head sharply, not expecting that question. She took a shaky breath, and her breasts pressed against the tank top. She could lie, but she wasn't going to. Brie figured this confession might be a good thing because they could get it all out in the open and stop pretending it wasn't obvious.

"Yes, Xander. I am very attracted to you." She let him know, and he smiled inwardly as his heartbeat increased at her words. Xander felt good at what she said, yet he wasn't going to act toward it. This could be something he could think about when he was in bed tonight… wishing she was next to him. He had an inkling on how she would respond and was glad her words had put his uncertainty at ease.

"If you're too shy to ask, I am attracted to you as well, Brie." She chuckled nervously, covering her mouth with her fingertips, rejoicing at his admission. This was the first time she had felt a mutual attraction with a man in a long time, and it was sad because it couldn't go any further. She wasn't going to put any crazy demands on him, and if she had the choice between his friendship and having a guilt-ridden liaison, she chose the former.

"I know that you're an honorable man and won't act on any feelings," she said in a small voice with a tiny smile, and he agreed with her. He hadn't looked away, and he thought he saw tears forming in her eyes.

"And I won't have you messing around with a married man."

"I don't want that either; for both our sakes. So for my peace of mind, let's just stay friends and not let this attraction mess up anything."

"Of course." As soon as Xander said that, the rain let up, but it didn't stop. It became tame enough where he could see and get back on the expressway. They didn't say anything to each other as they headed back toward Chicago; both in serious thought about what was just revealed. Silently acknowledging that there was no turning back from what they had shared.

Chapter 10

A few weeks later was the scholarship event, and everything was running on schedule for the night. After Xander had mentioned it to her, a representative from the planning committee had gotten in contact with Brie about having the event at the hotel. After speaking with her, they agreed to have it at Dynasty Towers, and Brie made sure her staff would be on hand to make it a successful night.

The dinner was to start at six p.m., and Brie stopped in the room a few times to see if anything was needed. Just before it began, Brie caught a glimpse of Xander in a tuxedo, looking so handsome and sexy. The dinner jacket fit him perfectly around his broad shoulders. He nodded at her, admiring how exquisite she looked in her royal-blue dress and gold heels. On her way out, she spotted Starr and didn't recognize her at first. She aged badly over the years, and Brie would've overlooked her if she hadn't spotted her on Xander's arm decked out in a green dress.

Marshall and Natalie were also in attendance; he in his tuxedo and she in her dazzling, red evening gown. The affair started on time, and the recipients and their families were so thrilled. Some of their classmates were there, and they were delighted that two NFL celebrities were emceeing. After the opening remarks, the two hosts spent time talking about each applicant and highlighted excerpts from their essay entries.

After being presented with a check and plaque, the young men gave short speeches, pictures were taken with the committee, and that ended the presentation segment of the evening. The night concluded with a fancy dinner, Cappuccino tarts, dancing, and merriment followed the rest of the night. Xander and Marshall both agreed that it had been a successful celebration. The former was talking to some of his frat brothers when his cell phone went off and saw it was his dad.

"Hey, Dad. What's up?" He listened to the call, pressing his free hand to his other ear. "Wait, what?" Xander's heart dropped as his dad repeated what he said; six words making him go cold.

"Your mother is in the hospital."

"Which one?" he asked, already heading toward Starr so they could leave.

Brie was at the front desk talking to the night desk clerk.

She had her purse with her and was about to grab something to eat when the banquet doors flew open. She looked on with worry and concern when Xander stormed out the room, dragging Starr behind him.

"What's wrong? What happened?" Brie asked Natalie and Marshall as they followed the first couple.

"We'll tell you on the way," Natalie replied as she ushered Brie to come with them.

****

Xander rushed through the emergency room doors of Ridgeview General Hospital, scanning the space for his father. He finally saw Xen pacing in the waiting area, and he ran to him.

"Dad! What the hell happened?" Xander asked as the four people gathered around.

"I-I don't know. She was making lasagna for dinner, and her hands turned red and had bumps on them. She collapsed when I bought her here and they're still working on her. I called you, and I just tried to get an update before you walked in, but they couldn't tell me anything yet." Xander walked away with his dad so they could speak privately. Brie was standing next to Natalie and Marshall, and they were looking troubled.

"Sounds like she had an allergic reaction," Marshall mumbled.

Starr looked around and frowned when she saw Brie talking to the Thorntons with a furrowed brow. She marched over to them with a hand on her hip. "Who are you?"

"Hey, Starr. I'm Brie."

"It's Mrs. Sterling to you. Why are you here?" Starr demanded.

"She's a friend, Starr. Chill out," Natalie spoke, and Starr rolled her eyes at her.

"I don't know you. Again, why are you here?" Brie didn't understand why Starr had an attitude and was being antagonistic toward her.

"We went to the same school, and I used to tutor Xander. S&T is doing contract work for me. I'm a friend, and I wanted to make sure everything was all right." Brie told her, and Starr looked her up and down before striding away and smacking her lips.

"She is unbelievable," Natalie whispered, and Brie agreed

with her.

The six people settled in cushioned, brown chairs in the glass-encased waiting area. There were other people occupying the space, but Xander wasn't paying them any attention. Brie checked her phone and saw it was after ten p.m. They had been waiting for more than thirty minutes and hadn't heard anything yet. Brie looked between Xander and his dad, seeing a strong resemblance.

Xen was handsome for his age, and she knew Xander would still be a looker in his older years. She wanted so much to wrap her arms around Xander to comfort him, but she knew that wasn't possible. What Brie didn't understand was why Starr wasn't by her husband's side. This was a scary moment in a person's life, and he needed her emotional support now. She looked at the woman and saw Starr on her phone; her fingers tapping away on her phone. *Is she playing a game?*

The wait continued, and the doctor still hadn't come out to speak to the Sterling men. Brie mentioned that she was going to get coffee for everyone and went to locate the cafeteria. Starr put her phone in her clutch and let out a deep breath in irritation. She stood up and went to the nurse's station. Xander was sitting next to Xen; neither saying a word, and they had uneasy expressions on their faces.

The Thorntons could understand their apprehension. Xander's parents had been together forever, and one couldn't function without the other. They knew the men felt helpless and wished there was something more they could do. Xen kept wondering and asking why he wasn't the one who had gotten sick and would easily trade places with his wife if it meant she would get better.

Starr came back in the sizable waiting area with a nonchalant manner and let out a bored sigh. "I just spoke with the nurse, and they're still working on Lola."

"So what? That's my wife in there, and the doctor can take all the time she needs!" Xen exclaimed, and she rolled her eyes again before turning her back on him.

"Xander, get your wife," Xen warned, as he stood up.

"Starr, are you fucking kidding me right now?" Xander asked as he grabbed her arm and pulled her away from the group into the hallway. He had a look in his eyes that she hadn't seen before. There was definite anger, fear, and rage, and she felt bad for causing more distress.

"I'm just saying, honey, we've been here for almost an hour and should've been told something by now."

"I don't give a damn how long it's been! Do you understand that is my mother in there, and you're out here acting like an ass?"

"Xander, don't—"

"Leave, Starr. Take the car and go," he said with disgust

She looked at him with wide eyes and grabbed the lapel of his jacket. "I'm sorry, honey. I'm just—"

"I don't care. You haven't asked one time how I am or tried to be supportive. Goodbye, Starr." He gave her the keys and marched away, not wanting to look at her right now. She took no time leaving the building, and Xander was glad she had left. He didn't want to deal with her and wasn't going to be responsible for what he said. Brie came back, carrying a cup holder with several coffee cups.

"Mr. Sterling, I have some decaf coffee if you want it. You probably don't need the caffeine to add to your nerves," she said softly, placing the cup on the table next to his chair.

"Thank you, Miss…"

"Calhoun. Brie Calhoun." Xen stood up again and began

pacing the floor. He hated hospitals and figured no news from the doctor was a good thing. Brie didn't see Starr around, and she looked at Natalie with question in her eyes. Her friend told her what happened, and she shook her head in annoyance. That wasn't right. She was supposed to be here for Xander. Unable to stop herself, she went to go sit next to him and placed her hand on his warm back.

"Hey."

"Hey," he said softly, undoing the bow tie and the top two buttons of his shirt.

"Your mom is going to be fine, Xander. They're just being meticulous to make sure she's going to be okay." He nodded, the heat from her hand calming his body minute by minute.

"Thanks, Brie," he muttered, rubbing a hand over his eyes.

A short Asian woman came into the waiting room with a clipboard in her hand, and she pushed up her glasses. "Mr. Sterling?"

Xen stood up and hurried over to her, and Xander stood beside his father. "I-I'm Lola's husband. How is she?"

"I'm Dr. Chu. Your wife is fine. It was a good thing you brought her to the hospital. She had an allergic reaction from the tomatoes and went into anaphylactic shock. She passed out because her blood pressure dropped, but I gave her a shot of Epinephrine to reverse the symptoms. We also gave her Fludrocortisone, which will bring her pressure back up. She's been admitted so we can monitor her for a few days." Dr. Chu reported, and Xander closed his eyes, glad to hear the good news. Brie saw the relief on Xen's face, and she smiled gently.

"Thank you so much, Dr. Chu. Is it common to develop allergies this late in life?" Xen quizzed in a concerned voice.

"Unfortunately, there is no time frame for allergic reactions. They can come and go at any age. Before she's discharged, I'm going to write a prescription for an EpiPen in case this happens again. Just make sure she stays away from tomatoes and anything related."

"I sure will. Can I see her?"

Dr. Chu nodded, and Xander said a quick farewell to his friends before he followed Xen. Brie waved at Xander and trailed the married couple out the hospital and was glad Xander's mom would be OK.

****

Three days later, Lola was back to her old self and was

discharged with aftercare instructions. Xen had filled her prescriptions, and Lola was perturbed she wouldn't be able to make her famous spaghetti again. Xen had told her it didn't matter because her health was more important than food. When Xander got home after leaving the hospital, his anger toward Starr had returned. Surprisingly, she was there, and when she asked about Lola's condition, he didn't answer. He went straight to his room and closed the door.

He had visited his mom in the hospital until she was well enough to go home. Monday morning, after she was discharged, Xander informed Marshall he was going to take some days off the job site to spend time with his mother, and his friend understood. Before he left, he went to the hotel and up to Brie's office and could hear her typing from the open door.

He knocked, and she looked up with a grin. "Hey, Xander," she greeted him and stood up to wave him in.

"Hi, Brie. I didn't mean to disturb you," he declared, and she waved a hand at him.

"It's fine. I'm leaving in a few minutes. I'm here, but I'm not here."

"Are you heading home?"

"No. Natalie wants to go hang out today. How is your mom doing?"

"Mom is fine. Thank you for asking. She's at home resting. I'm heading that way now when I leave here. I... um... I wanted to thank you for being there for me at the hospital."

"You don't have to thank me, Xander. We're friends, right? I'm just glad your mom is doing better. I know your dad is feeling better about the situation. How is he?"

Xander nodded and chuckled. "He is, and he's fine. That's one of the reasons why I'm going over there, I think he's driving my mom crazy."

Brie smiled at that. "He's just being cautious. I know she'll be happy to see you."

Xander nodded and cleared his throat. He wanted to say more to her, but he didn't know what. Brie watched him with tender eyes and wanted to give him a hug; a friend-appropriate hug. She knew the past few days had been stressful and filled with fear over his mom. If she had been in that same situation, she would worry about her parent as well.

On the way over, Xander realized just how remarkable Brie was. She was great at the hospital by being there and offering kind words. He tried to fight his fascination toward her, but it was not working.

"Are you good, Xander?"

"Yeah. I'm going to go. Take care, Brie,"

She jerked her head and went with him to the door. Xander stopped at the exit and took a deep breath, throwing his head back. "I tried. Damnit, I tried," he insisted softly.

"Tried to do—" Before Brie could finish her question, in a flash, Xander had pushed her against the wall, lowered his head, and they were finally embraced in a kiss.

Chapter 11

The moment his lips touched hers, Brie's world stopped, and nothing else mattered at that point. She didn't try to stop it or think about if it was right or wrong. She selfishly and greedily mated with his lips, and sweet Lord, it was good! Xander's mouth was soft and determined as his tongue made its way inside her mouth. He had a taste that she could bask in forever, and it had a citrus tang. Her fingers squeezed his biceps that were pressing against his shirt; his arms feeling solid and safe. Xander knew the second he had her lips, it was over for him. The kiss was slow, comforting, and it matched how she made him feel.

Tongues caressed the opposite one, and mouths were being nibbled and sucked on. They both had wondered how a kiss would be between them, but it was nothing like the provocative one that was going on now. It was heaven, raw, and passionate. Xander couldn't remember the last time a kiss got him going like this, and he didn't want it to end.

Brie gasped in her throat when he grabbed her ass and did a combo move of lifting and pressing her against the front of his pants; his hands fingering the shape of her booty as he squeezed it. One of her legs curled around his thigh as her arms circled his neck. Her nipples got hard and became visible against her tank top. Xander let out an unruly moan at her touch, and his skin craved it.

Xander didn't bother to hide his aching erection. He couldn't do anything about it, and he was content with having her clothed body snuggled against his. Brie swiped her tongue over his bottom lip before he stood up to his full height and touched his forehead to hers. She pinched her mouth together to keep his essence on her, and he kept his hands on her behind.

They stood together taking in the ambience, and he swore he could smell her arousal trickling from her pores. It took every speck of willpower he had to not take things further, and he let out a shaky breath.

"Thank you." He breathed against her lips before leaving the office. Brie went to the couch and sat down on unsteady legs. No kiss had ever rendered her speechless and screaming for release like the one she shared with Xander. She ran her thumb over her swollen lips and closed her eyes at the tenderness.

****

Twelve days after that dazzling, perfect kiss, everything was back to the way it was before, but it was hard to concentrate on things from their perspective. They found themselves daydreaming about that kiss, wondering if and when it would happen again. But Brie knew it was wishful thinking, and Xander tried to convince himself it was a kiss of gratitude, but he knew that was a lie.

She visited the construction site; her first since the lamp accident. Brie had walked through with caution, seeing the addition to the floors, and she had asked questions about the project. Marshall and Xander took turns answering her questions, and she tried to not drool on herself when she saw Xander working with no shirt on that day. He had a slim waist with a six-pack and a trail of hair under his belly button that disappeared behind his belt, and she wanted to lick that patch of hair until he moaned. He was still toned, athletic, and was undeniably fine as hell. Xander looked at her with wanting and desire, and she tried to ignore it.

Brie left for the day after that. She felt like she was about to go crazy and needed some time away from Xander. After spending another night tossing and turning, she ended up oversleeping the next morning and hurried out the door after a quick shower. Xander had called her when she got in the car to tell her about the landscapers she asked them about. They were looking to meet with her, and Brie told him she would speak to him about it once she got to the hotel.

Brie was sitting at the light on 53rd and Lake Park and waiting for it to turn green so she could stop at her favorite café to get a cup of coffee. It had been hot the last few days, but it was a gloomy day today, and it smelled like rain was on the way. Getting the green arrow to turn left, Brie started to move when she heard tires screech and didn't recall anything after a tan minivan plowed into the right side of her car.

****

Xander hurried through the doors of the University of Chicago Hospital emergency room. He had rushed there after getting a call from a nurse Vivian about Brie being in a car accident. She had called the last number from Brie's phone, and Xander was glad he had answered. After tracking down the nurse, he identified himself, and she took him to where Brie was resting in a curtained area. Brie's eyes were closed and from what he could see, she looked pretty banged up. There was a big bandage on her left temple, scratches on her face, and her right ankle was wrapped up.

"What are you doing here?" Qyle demanded, irritated that he had shown up. She was sitting in the chair next to the bed and jumped up when he approached them. She knew Brie had feelings for Xander and didn't want her friend to be hurt by him. She knew Brie would never mess around with him, but she didn't know or trust Xander.

"I got a call from a nurse about the car accident, and I came right over. Is she OK?" he asked, walking closer to the bed; his heart going at an erratic beat.

"She's fine. She's sleeping from the pain medicine they gave her, and I'm waiting for them to come back with her X-rays." Xander looked at Brie again, and Qyle didn't like it.

"How did you know she was here?" Xander questioned her.

"The nurse called me when she couldn't get in contact with Theo. Although I don't know why you were called," Qyle said the last part loud and clear, and Xander got pissed.

"Ask the nurse why I was called, not that it matters."

"You can leave, Xander. I'll take care of Brie," she told him in a dismissive nature, and he frowned.

"What the hell is your problem, Qyle?"

"My problem is you're a married man sniffing around my best friend."

"Brie is my friend, and that was long before you two met. I don't know why you're staking your claim on her, but I just wanted to make sure she was OK."

"She is. You can go now." Xander let out a low growl and left.

Brie was discharged hours later with strict orders from the doctor to be on bed rest for the next few days. Qyle drove her home and helped her get settled on the couch so she could relax. She put a glass of water on the table next to her prescriptions and placed a small afghan over her. Brie's white shirt had some blood drops on it, and Qyle placed her swollen ankle on a pillow.

"Are you sure you want me to leave, Brie? I can stay and reschedule my trip."

"I'm fine, Qyle. I'm just going to sleep it off," Brie said softly, grimacing from her sore ribs, and her voice was hoarse.

Qyle sighed and stood up straight. "I'll be back in a few days and will call to check up on you." Brie nodded and laid back on the couch and was asleep before Qyle locked the door behind her.

Hours later, Brie gasped as she shifted to her right side; the pain causing her to wake up. It was dark outside, and the house was quiet. The windows were open, and she snuggled against her afghan. She saw her phone sitting on the floor by the couch, and she sluggishly reached for it. The battery was low, and she had fourteen missed calls; two from Qyle, and the rest were from Xander. She called her friend back and ended up leaving a voicemail. She returned Xander's call next, and he picked up on the first ring.

"Brie?"

"Hi, Xander." She returned, clearing her dry throat.

"I'm glad you called. I was about to jump in my truck and head over there. Are you all right?"

"Yeah, I fell asleep from the meds after I got home and just woke up."

"Feel better?" he asked with nervousness.

"I haven't eaten yet, so I'm going to see what's in the

kitchen."

"Say no more. I'll bring you some food," he vowed.

"No, Xander. It's late, and you don't have to."

"It's only nine. I know you probably don't eat this late, but you need to put something on your stomach."

"I don't know about—"

"I'll only stay for a few minutes. I just need to see you and make sure you're really OK," he said more to reassure himself than trying to persuade her.

"I am, Xander." Her voice was calm, yet he could hear the fragility in it.

"I need to see for myself." She sighed, grimacing at her sore ribs again. She agreed, and he was happy to hear that she acquiesced.

"Good, I'm on my way. There is a diner a few blocks from me, and I'll grab you something from there."

"There are some rocks under the rosebush in front of the house. There is a spotted one in the back; it's fake, and there is a spare key hidden inside."

"Do you need anything else, Brie?"

"No, I'm fine. Thank you for asking."

They hung up, and Brie took her time sitting up, waiting for the dizziness to pass. She tried to rotate her ankle but wheezed at the pain. She was glad to have walked away with minor injuries, especially after Qyle told her how badly her vehicle ended up. She knew it would be a few days before she could move around without any stiffness, and she'd deal with the insurance company tomorrow.

Brie called Elmo to update him since she knew Qyle had called him earlier that day. After endless questions, he told her to get some rest, and he'd take care of things at the hotel. She hung up and was attempting to shimmy off the couch when her father called.

"Hey, Daddy."

"Brie! Are you OK? We just docked in Sydney, and my messages finally came through. I got a voicemail from Qyle saying you'd been in a car accident." His tone was urgent and filled with worry.

"I was, but I'm fine, Dad."

"Well, what the hell happened?" She relayed the accident to him, and he listened intently. Brie then heard her father's words and tears fell down her face.

"I know, Dad… yeah… I'll take care of it… No, you don't have to fly home," she said the last part with a smile, wiping her eyes.

"You sure? You know I'll ditch this boat for you."

"I'm fine. I already spoke to Elmo, and he's got everything covered. I'm going to spend the next few days recuperating."

"You better. If you need anything, call me."

"Daddy, you're on the other side of the world. If I did need anything, how are you going to bring it to me?"

"Don't be a smart aleck. Get some rest, honey."

"I will. Have fun in Australia." They disconnected, and she wiped her face again. She heard the door knob jingle and saw Xander walk in. She was glad he had shown up and was relieved to see him. He placed the food bag on the dining room table and strolled towards her.

Xander sat next to her on the couch, his hands going to her face where his thumbs softly caressed the underside of her swollen, bruised jaw. He was careful to avoid the fresh scratches and hoped he wasn't hurting her. Brie closed her eyes and curved her head toward his touch. The pain didn't seem so bad when his hands were on her, and she didn't want it to end. Xander wanted to kiss her again right then, but knew it wasn't an appropriate time.

"Are you really OK, Brie?" he asked again, and she nodded.

"I'm just sore. Did you come from work?" she wondered, taking in his attire of black trousers and a black-and-gray patterned shirt with no tie.

"No, I came from home."

"Xander—"

"Shh, it's fine. Do you need anything?"

"Actually, yes. I wanted to take a bath before I ate," she stated, and he nodded. "Consider it done."

"Xander, you—"

"Can you get off the couch, walk upstairs, and run the bath water yourself?"

"No, but—"

"But nothing. Let me take care of things while I'm here." Brie knew he was being nice, but there was something about him being in her bathroom and touching her things that made it so intimate and personal. If he was like this as a friend, she could picture how he was as a husband. She watched him take his shoes off and jogged upstairs.

Xander didn't bother looking at the neatly-made queen-sized bed that was decorated in lavender and gold. The bathroom was large with a claw-style tub that had a curved back and a glass shower sat across from the bath. He turned on the hot water and poured in some bubble bath. Then he went back downstairs and let her brace herself before he lifted her off the couch. She closed her eyes and bit her bottom lip, whimpering in pain.

"I'm sorry," he uttered, and she nodded. The tub was slowly filling when he placed her on the bench against the wall across from the mirror. After he gathered towels, Xander bent down and unwrapped her puffy ankle. It was red, swollen, and ugly looking, and he wished he thought to get some Epsom salt.

While she was bathing, Xander had placed the pancakes and bacon he bought on a red tray in the kitchen with a cup of orange juice and carried it to her room. When she emerged minutes later, Xander rushed to help Brie to the bed, which he had turned down. Hot shivers ran up her skin as he swathed her ankle again and placed two pillows under it for elevation.

"Do you want some?" she asked him, pointing to the food.

"No, I'm good. I already ate."

She drank some juice and looked at him. "Thank you for doing this." Xander stared at her, taking in her features before speaking.

"You're welcome. Do you want to take another pain pill?"

"No, not right now. They make me sleepy." He glanced at the TV and saw her adjust her terry robe out the corner of his eye.

"Before I left the hospital, I found out about the driver of the other car. It was a teenager with a learner's permit. He ran the light and hit you." Xander reported, and Brie was stunned.

"Was he hurt badly?"

Xander shook his head and settled back onto the window seat. "He had a few bumps and bruises. It was good neither of you sustained worse injuries." Brie agreed with that, and they talked for two hours before he left. Xander made her promise to call him if she needed anything, and she said she would.

Brie rested for a week and ended up asking Xander to take her to the junkyard so she could take pictures of her totaled car for insurance purposes and had to get a copy of the police report. She would've asked Qyle, but she was still away on business, and it needed to be taken care of right away. When she finally got back to the hotel, she had a pile of paperwork waiting for her. She was glad to be back and found out that a lot of rooms had been reserved for a cheerleading competition. After receiving a warm welcome from her employees, Brie went to her office to catch up on things.

Chapter 12

Xander was in the basement of his house, huffing and puffing as he used the workout equipment. He was sporting a pair of sweats with no shirt, and he was lifting weights. It was a Friday afternoon, and he had left work after putting in a few hours. As usual, he was working off his sexual frustration and irritation that he couldn't talk to Brie without a reason. He never thought he'd be a married man suffering from blue balls. It had now been over ten months since his last physical encounter with Starr, and he didn't care about having sex with her anymore. He wanted Brie in a bad way but promised himself he wouldn't touch her again as a married man.

He sat up and let out a deep breath as sweat ran down his flat stomach at an unhurried drip. The muscles in his arms were glistening from the exertion, and he felt like he had a good workout. As he was slipping on his tank top, he heard the front door open and voices echoing through the empty house with several footsteps. The basement door was open, and he could hear Starr talking to Casey, but what he wasn't expecting was to hear two male voices he didn't recognize.

"Are you sure this is cool? Your husband's truck is in the

198

driveway. He could be upstairs," one of the males said.

"It's fine. He's not here. He uses the company truck for work. Let's go outside."

The patio door was slid open, and Xander walked to the window that faced the backyard. He saw a black man and white man standing by his wife and Casey. They were short, and the latter had a bulging stomach. Starr turned on the hot tub that was built into the porch and was hidden from the neighbors. The black guy had his hands all over Casey, and she was smiling like a kid on Christmas.

Xander pulled out his cell phone from his pants pocket and began to record them with his camera. He watched as the four of them talked for a few minutes; his hand balling into a fist when he saw Starr and the white man giving each other sexual pats here and there. He looked on with disgust, unadulterated anger, and unbelievability when the two women undid the men's pants and bent down to perform oral sex.

He could not believe what he was seeing. He always had an inkling that Starr was cheating on him, but to see it with his own eyes was something unexpected. From his position, he had a clear view of Starr and could see she was enjoying herself and what she was doing.

"You cheating bitch! We'll see who gets the last laugh." Xander recorded thirty more seconds of evidence that showed them switching partners then left the basement. He managed to grab his keys and leave the house without being seen. He drove without the radio on, replaying what he just witnessed in his own goddamn house that he paid for. He knew where he was heading, and he was glad that soon he'd be free from that cheating ass wife of his.

****

"This is... wow." Xander's lawyer, a middle-aged black man named Glenn Seamus, sat down at his desk, looking at the video of Starr. Glenn had been Xander's lawyer since his football days and had an office in Barrington. He was the same height as Xander, a confirmed bachelor, and had a bald spot in the middle of his head. He was in his early fifties and had a full, bushy beard. Xander was staring out the window of the air-conditioned office, not really looking at anything. On his way to Mr. Seamus's office, Xander had taken off his wedding ring and tossed it out the window. He didn't want anything reminding him of Starr and their atrocious marriage.

"I'm sorry to barge in like this," Xander said, turning to face the older man, his hands in his pockets.

"It's fine, Xander." Glenn put the phone down and looked at his young client, empathizing with him. That was a hellafied way to find out your wife was cheating on you.

"It's pretty obvious, but what do you want to do, Xander?"

"Start the divorce proceedings today. I'm done with Starr."

Glenn reached for his pen and began making notes on a notepad. "She might contest the divorce."

"She can do whatever she wants. I don't care, Glenn."

"I'll get the paperwork started."

"I want this done fast," Xander stated firmly.

"I'll do my best. Can you come back to get your phone later? I need to transfer the video to a disc as a backup."

Xander agreed and left the office. Ten days later, the papers had been delivered to Starr, who was blindsided. A few days after Xander visited his lawyer, he had gone home to pack his things and left the house he shared with her. Starr hadn't been home when he left, and he was glad for that. He ended up checking into the W hotel downtown, which was good because it was close to the office and job site.

He also made an appointment to see his doctor to get tested for STD's. He was calm as he waited for the results since they hadn't had sex in several months, but he wanted to be sure. Xander had shown Marshall the recording, and his friend had no words. They had talked for hours in Marshall's home, and Xander told him about the divorce.

"To hell with Starr. You don't need her."

"I know. I just feel a sense of relief because now I don't have to wonder, and I can move on with my life."

His conversation with Marshall was two days ago, and Xander felt like a weight had been lifted off his chest regarding his marriage. It was unfortunate it would have to end this way, but there was no other option. Now all Starr had to do was sign the papers, and they could go their separate ways. He was at the office filling out some papers when Starr stormed in. He could tell she was mad, and tears were running down her face.

"Xander! What is the meaning of this?" she asked him, holding up the folded papers.

"You can read, Starr. You know damn well what it is," he

replied, sitting back in the chair.

"Is this because I didn't make it to the counseling session? I apologized about that, Xander. I told you I—"

"I don't want to hear it. Just sign the papers and be done with it."

She threw the documents at him, and he caught them with one hand. "I'm not signing them. I love you, honey. Please, let's talk about this," she pleaded, walking further into the room.

"You weren't thinking about me or our marriage when you were giving some dude a blow job in my house, were you?" Xander saw the color drain from her face, and she felt her heart skip a beat.

He knew! Starr closed her eyes and took a deep, shuddering breath as fresh tears ran down her cheeks. "Xander…"

"Save it, Starr! Your dirt finally caught up with you, so deal with the consequences. Hear me good, I do not want to be married to you anymore. Now sign the damn papers." Xander stood up and rested his fists on his desk.

Her facial features changed into a hard mask, and she

wiped her tears away with a defiant hand. "Do you think I'm going to let you divorce me? It's your fault I'm like this, Xander, and you're going to pay."

He stalked over to her, but she kept her ground, and she tossed her chin up. "It's my fault you're out here sucking on random dick? Yeah, see how that plays out in front of a judge. And in case you forgot, you signed a prenup, so you might want to save what little money you have left."

Starr made a loud screeching noise at that and slapped Xander across his face before storming out the room. He shook his head at her dramatics and went back to the desk. He couldn't believe that she blamed him for her infidelities, and he realized the sooner this was over with, the better.

****

The next day, Brie was walking into the hotel when she saw Marshall coming out the restaurant with a cup of coffee and a box of pastries. It was one of those rare summer days where the temperature would stay in the eighties, making it perfect weather for people to appreciate the city.

"Good morning, Marshall."

"Morning, Brie. I'm glad to see you're back to your

regular self after that accident."

She thanked him, and they made small talk for a few seconds, but she had to inquire about his business partner before he headed next door.

"Marshall... um, I'm probably overstepping my boundaries, but is Xander alright? I've tried to call him a few times, and he hasn't returned any of my calls or messages," she confessed softly, and he looked at her with understanding.

"He's OK, but not OK. He's going through something serious right now."

She acknowledged him, her pulse beating faster at what Marshall had just said. "But he is well? He's not hurt or anything?" He assured her again and folded her arms over her stomach,

"Thanks. I won't hold you up. Have a good day."

She headed to her office and glanced at her phone when it went off and saw it was a text message from Faith. *Working on something big for the hotel. Will let you know of the details later.* Brie wondered what that was about as she sat down to turn on the computer. She was glad today was Thursday since she had one more work day and would be off for the weekend.

She'd dealt with a hotel full of teenage girls all week during the cheerleading event, and they had kept the place rowdy. After messaging Qyle back to confirm their dinner plans for tonight, she started the work day by checking her emails.

Next door, Marshall set a level against a wall and adjusted it as Xander grabbed his hammer. The crew had been given their duties for the day, and construction noises could be heard with the sounds of the radio.

"Brie asked about you this morning," Marshall told his friend, who didn't say anything as he hit the wall. Xander missed the hell out of Brie but felt it best to keep his distance.

He hadn't heard from Starr since her office visit and got an email from Glenn to confirm he hadn't heard anything from Starr's attorney yet. Xander also received a call from his physician to let him know he was great as far as his health, and his tests had come back negative. He still had a tan line on his finger from the wedding band, but the skin wasn't clammy like it had been when he yanked the ring off. Xander kept the day professional and was glad that work kept his mind from wandering to the woman he wanted to see the most.

****

The next night, Xander was leaning against the wall next to the window in his hotel room watching the rain fall. He could see numerous cars on Lake Shore Drive, and the drizzle wasn't stopping people from going on with their evening. He had gotten something to eat when he got off work and went straight to the hotel. That was two hours ago, and he was still thinking about everything that had occurred.

Xander had bitten the bullet and told his parents that he was filing for a divorce but didn't go into detail about the video. Not that they would add fuel to the fire, but he didn't feel like dealing with his mother's endless questions and didn't want to see their knowing looks neither. It was after nine p.m., and he was feeling antsy. Not because he wanted to go out, but because he wanted to see Brie. He always said he wouldn't touch her as a married man and technically, he still was. But given the circumstances, he felt like that shouldn't stop him from going to see her and talk. Xander grabbed his keys and left the hotel with determined steps.

In her townhouse, Brie was sitting in the window seat in her bedroom with a glass of red wine on the table next to her. The rain had bought an uncomfortable mugginess with it, so the AC was on to balance that feeling. The radio was on the R&B station at a low volume, and the DJ was playing slow jams. Her right leg was lying straight, and her left leg was bent at the knee. She had showered and had on a teal night shirt with nothing underneath.

She had yet to hear from Xander and hoped everything was well with him. She could tell this would be another night where she'd use her vibrator, even though she wished for a flesh-and-blood substitute. While out to dinner with Qyle, she had mentioned that she met someone, but was taking things slow with a girl named Emma. She was glad to hear her friend was dating and hoped she was good to Qyle. Brie's heart jumped when her doorbell rang, interrupting the peaceful mood of the house. She wasn't expecting anyone and wasn't up for company. She gasped when she saw Xander through the peephole standing on the stoop. Unlocking the door, she opened it, but before she could greet him, Xander pushed through the door and bent down to kiss her.

Chapter 13

At first, it was raw, urgent, and untamed as Xander initiated it, and she eagerly participated. It then slowed down to a tender kiss as one hand caressed her cheek, and the other gripped her hip while her arms locked around his waist. He pressed her against the wall; easing up on the embrace when Brie whimpered in her throat. It converted to a lingering, consuming, delicious kiss, and Xander felt like he was about to lose his mind when she suckled on his tongue. Her nipples became like daggers against the shirt, and she inhaled sharply when he cupped her left breast; his thumb moving over her tantalizing flesh.

"Xander..." she muttered, patting him on his chest; her weak attempt to push him away wasn't working.

"I'm sorry... I had to..." He lowered his head down to her neck and pecked at the area behind her ear. His mouth felt so good, and she didn't want him to stop. She ran her hands up his warm back and took her time feeling the dips and slopes of his extensive frame. His hands stole under her shirt and slowly circled the shape of her ass.

"Xander, we can't..." Brie pulled her lips from his after

several unsuccessful attempts. Her body was feverishly hot, and her breath was coming out in shaky sounds. He straightened up but didn't step away; his breathing coming out just as ragged. Xander reached up and ran his thumb over her plumb bottom lip that was damp from his mouth.

"I had to see you, Brie."

"Is everything OK?" she asked, frowning at his declaration.

"It is now." Xander felt like a big stone had lifted from his shoulders now that he was here, and he closed his eyes when she trailed her fingers down his face. He lifted his left hand, and she saw his wedding ring was gone. Brie clasped his hand as she stroked the pale skin.

"What happened?" she whispered to him.

"It's a long story, and I'll give you the cliff notes later. It's over, Brie. For good."

Brie was astonished to hear the news, wondering how that came to pass, but she wasn't going to pry. "What are you going to do now?" she asked as their fingers interlocked.

He moved closer to her and lowered his head. They nibbled at each other's lips again, basking in the mating of

210

their mouths. Xander kissed his way to her ear and told her what he was going to do to her. She got as far as, *take you upstairs and put my tongue...* before her legs turned to jelly, and he wrapped his arm around her waist to keep her upright. She rested her head against his chest and gave in. She was tired of fighting this attraction and didn't have the strength anymore. She was so wet and quivering between her legs.

"Do you want that too, Brie?" he asked, gently biting her earlobe, his breath tickling the damp skin.

"You can't expect me to think right now when you're doing that," she replied breathlessly, and he chuckled.

"I can't help it. You smell good. Answer my question, Brie." She viewed him; their eyes meeting in silent understanding. If she said no, that would be fine. He'd just have to take the world's coldest shower. Xander didn't want her to feel pressured, but her silence was killing him. He had felt her naked skin and the weight of her ample breasts, and he wanted so much more.

"Take your shoes off," she ordered, and he complied without hesitation. Brie grabbed his hand and led him in the direction of her bedroom. In the hallway, Brie stopped walking when he grabbed her from behind. He snaked an arm around her belly, pushed her hair to the side and began kissing the back of her neck.

She moaned loudly, pushing her behind against his bulging erection. She was liking what she was feeling and couldn't wait to see it up close. Brie cupped his head from behind, her body yelling in ecstasy. His free hand went under her shirt and he slowly palmed the inside of her thighs close to her honeypot.

"Xander, please," she begged, turning to the right to connect her lips with his. Somehow, they made it to the bedroom, she switched their positions, and shoved him toward the bed. Brie yanked his T-shirt off and threw it on the floor. He had on a white tank top under it, and he looked so yummy in it.

She fingered his muscled arms, loving the strength and hardness of them. Xander sat on the edge of the bed, and she could see his dick pressing against his jeans.

"Brie—" he stopped when she pulled off his undershirt, "I have a clear head about this. I don't have any conflicting feelings about—" She placed two fingers on his lips to stop him from speaking.

"I know, Xander. I have a clear mind too. I won't regret this." She confirmed, and he licked the digits.

Xander reached for her and got rid of the thin shirt. She watched as his patient eyes perused her naked body and sighed in anticipation. "You are exquisite." He revealed, and her heart turned over. He gathered Brie to him, cupped her head, and started kissing her delectable lips.

It felt so perfect to finally have their bare flesh touching. The springy hair on his chest tickled her heated skin, and it caused her nipples to become firm again. Breaking the kiss, he lowered his head and took one of them into his hot mouth as he fingered the breast he was tending to.

She closed her eyes after she realized he was going to take his time and not rush things with her. He was enjoying the texture and size of her nipples by using the flat side of his tongue and teeth to gently bite the protruding skin. Xander was shifting between her generous mounds, and she got lightheaded from the ministrations; her fingers lovingly running over his scalp.

Xander turned them around so Brie was on the bed, and

she sat back as he undid his pants. She watched with greedy desire when his nakedness was revealed. His legs and thighs were long and sinewy, and she could see the power in them. But what took her breath away was the bulbous, long, and thick dick standing at full mass, and he damn near shattered when he saw her lick her lips.

"You're bigger than I imagined." She pointed out as he ambled toward the bed, reaching for her smooth leg. Xander smiled that grin that she loved, and he situated himself between her legs with his eyes centered on her dewy middle.

"I can't wait to taste you," Xander spoke before bowing his head to take her. She closed her eyes and gasped with bliss as he marked her clit with his tongue. He wasn't going to be like some horny teenager and rush through this. He had been waiting to do this for a while, and after months of no sexual relations, he wanted to make sure he would be able to recall every detail afterward.

He held her warm thighs apart with his big hands, and she could hear him licking and suckling on her. Words escaped Brie, and her mind focused on what was being done to her as she reached down to cradle the back of his head. High-pitched, deep moans escaped from her, and she didn't try to stifle the sounds.

Brie's scent was driving Xander crazy. It wasn't flowery or fruity. It was more of a natural essence, and he wanted to sink into it. When he slid two slim fingers inside her wet channel, she arched her back and sharply inhaled between her teeth. His nonstop attention to her saturated vagina had her hips involuntary twirling on the bed from his mouth and touch. She hadn't had the good stuff yet, but this was way better than the vibrator.

She was arching and twisting and shuffling so much that the comforter became dislodged from its tucked in position, and the cold air was not doing a good job in cooling down her fevered skin. She curled her fingers around her left breast and squeezed it to incorporate with their foreplay. Brie could tell Xander was a man who enjoyed pleasing his woman in every way, and she couldn't wait to return the favor. He thought he would bust a nut when she creamed from her orgasm; her increased heartbeats making her pant out loud. Xander reared up and quickly put on a condom; needing to bury himself within her right now. He would've been fine with just sampling her pussy longer, but he wanted to feel her wrapped around him.

"Xander, I want to—"

"Later." He interrupted, supporting himself over her. They were laying along the short end of the bed, and she opened her legs to him. Brie watched his face as he guided inside her heat. She gulped and coiled her back to take him all in; Xander leaning down to nibble at her mouth. He started a gradual back and forth motion, and he growled when her nails pawed his back. Oh, my... This was so much better than she ever dreamed of, and it was what she's been wanting and craving.

Xander increased his moves, and that made her more excited. She cupped his flexing buttocks, and he lifted her calves to drive deeper into her tightness. She nicked his bottom lip; liking the grunting noises he was making in her ear. Despite the air, their bodies still produced a cool sweat film, and she urged him to keep going. He was trying like hell to not have a fast release, but when she was milking him, it wreaked havoc on his brain. Brie locked her legs around his waist and pulled him closer, which caused their chests to bump against the other. Brie kissed Xander to match his mighty pounces as they rode the waves of pleasure and wonder together.

****

The next morning, the air was still on to keep the townhouse cool from the summer heat. The weather report had confirmed that the weekend would bring temperatures in the mid-nineties, and Brie was prepared to keep the unit running all day and night. The couple was sleeping on their left sides, naked under the sheet with his hand resting on her hip. After their first sexual episode, it had taken minutes for them to get back at it. They both had a lot of saved up sexual vigor inside, and they were more than eager to let it out.

The third time they had sex, Brie ended up on top of Xander and had ridden him long and so damn magnificently. Xander was certain he would cherish the memory of her bouncing breasts and passion-laded face engraved in his mind. Brie's cell phone went off, but she didn't hear it. After another call and back-to-back messages, she opened her eyes and the phone rang again.

She saw it was after ten and reached for her phone to see who was blowing it up. She noticed Faith's number and texted her friend back: *Still sleep, what's up?* Faith responded for Brie to call her back as soon as possible, and Brie sighed, reclining back in the bed; wanting to get back to Xander's warmth. The phone chimed again, and Brie frowned as she read another message from Faith: *It's been three minutes. Muy importante!*

Brie managed to get out of bed; her inner muscles sore in a good way. She went to the bathroom to freshen up and placed an unopened toothbrush and face towel on the nightstand next to Xander before walking downstairs. She wanted nothing more than to wake him up so they could continue from last night, but apparently, that wasn't going to happen. Brie sat at the dining room table and returned Faith's call.

"OK, you're calling me back-to-back. Is everything all right with you?"

"Yes, and I have good news. I started shooting a new movie recently. It's an action picture, and I'm playing a spy. They're looking for a hotel on location with a certain look for the hotel-meeting and gun-fight scene, and I suggested Dynasty Towers," Faith told her friend with excitement in her voice.

"What did you just say?" Brie asked breathlessly; her heart thumping at the news.

"The movie studio is thinking about using your hotel for the movie. I was explaining how close it is to the lake, and the director and producers started talking about adding a helicopter escape to the scene, and the penthouse would be perfect as far as space. You're probably going to get a call from the location scout manager to schedule a meeting."

"Oh my God! That is exciting Faith! Thank you for suggesting the hotel. I didn't know they took recommendations from the actors with anything like that." Brie wasn't sure how the movie business worked and knew those with a big budget took time and patience to make sure their cinematic vision was seen by the movie lovers.

"I've worked with some of the crew members before and offered ideas in the past."

"That is awesome. Where are you now?"

"At home. We don't shoot on the weekends. You sound weird… different," Faith said, and Brie got quiet.

Upstairs, Xander was having a dream about last night and

woke up with a hard-on. He saw he was alone in the untidy bed, sat up, and saw the toiletries waiting for him. Xander walked into the bathroom naked and freshened up before locating Brie.

"I'm good, Faith." Brie informed as she got out the ingredients to make French toast and bacon.

"Uh huh. I'm getting a vibe from you." She laughed as she added eggs to the milk in a bowl. "Will you let me know if the studio calls you?"

Brie replied to Faith's question and hung up after chatting for a few minutes. She wasn't one to sleep in late but knew she had slept well because Xander had put it on her in more ways than one. She went in the living room to turn on the TV before opening a pack of bacon. She was sprinkling cinnamon and brown sugar on the first batch when Xander approached from behind and wrapped his arms around her.

"Good morning." She chuckled, touching his arm.

"Morning, gorgeous. I see you throwing down in here. It smells good."

"It's just a quick breakfast for us," she said kindly on a hitched breath as he tenderly bit her ear and was fingering her nipples over her shirt. Brie turned to face him and raised on her tip toes to touch her lips to his. Xander braced his hands on the counter behind her as they kept kissing one another. He wasn't imagining things; Brie's mouth and tongue were just as delicious as the night before.

"What caused you to leave me in the bed by myself?" She told him of the discussion she had with Faith, and he stepped back to stare at her.

"Really? That is great news," he responded with his hands on her hips.

"I know, but I won't get my hopes up high until I hear from them." He lowered his head again, and her hand moved down to stroke him through his boxers. Even flaccid, Xander still had an incredible package, and she liked fondling him.

"You probably want me to eat the food you made, huh?" Brie nodded and smiled against his mouth. "Then stop doing that."

She pulled back and licked her top lip. "Later?"

"Absolutely." They sat at the glass table in the dining room to have breakfast and coffee. After finishing her meal, Brie cleared her throat and observed Xander. He was shirtless at the table, and she wanted to relish every inch of his chest.

"So last night…"

"Yeah, about that… How do you feel?" Xander knew she said she wouldn't have any regrets, but he needed to hear her say the words.

"I feel good, Xander. What about you?"

"I feel damn great. In fact, I feel better than I have in months."

"Do you want to talk about what led you here? What happened with Starr?" Xander drank the last of his coffee before answering. He really didn't want to discuss it, but he knew Brie deserved the truth.

"I caught her cheating on me in our home, and I filed for divorce that day. I also packed my things and left." Brie was stunned to hear that; feeling frustrated and bothered for Xander's sake. He was a good man and didn't deserve what his wife had put him through.

She reached for his hand and gave it a comforting squeeze. "I'm sorry, Xander."

"It's not your fault," he said in a dismissive tone, and she knew it wasn't directed toward her.

"What will you do now?"

"I'm waiting on her to sign the papers so I can get on with my life," he answered honestly, and she let out a deep breath. Brie didn't know what to say about Starr's infidelity but knew he didn't warrant that behavior from her. On a different subject, Brie wanted Xander to stay with her today, but she didn't want to be too forward.

"Is what happened between us last night going to be a one-time thing?" Brie probed, giving him the side eye.

"Hell no! Brie, I've wanted you for months. You know why I applied restraint, but now that I've had you, I want more. A lot more," Xander proclaimed, and she started to twinge between her legs. She inhaled deeply, causing her breasts to move against her shirt, and it caught Xander's eye.

"Are you staying?"

"Do you want me to?" Brie nodded, and he grinned, sitting back in the leather chair. "Then I'll stay, but I have to get some clothes from my hotel room. I'm pretty sure you don't want me wearing the same pair of underwear the whole weekend."

"I understand," she said, standing up to take their plates into the kitchen. Xander caught her wrists and pulled her to

223

him, and she wrapped her arms around his head as he was still sitting down. They were quiet as she continued to embrace him and massage his scalp with her fingers.

"I'll make dinner tonight," he announced, and she was pleased at the news.

"That'll be nice. I didn't know you knew how to cook."

"Baby, it's things about me you couldn't imagine." That got Brie excited, and she gave him a peck on his forehead. After Xander got dressed, he made a shopping list and left the townhouse. As soon as he departed, Brie cleaned the kitchen, and after loading the dishwasher, she went upstairs and turned on the shower.

Sitting on the bed, a delightful smile swept across her face. Last night was totally unexpected and amazing at the same time. Xander had touched her in ways and spots she didn't know she had. While on top, Brie had to take it easy when she settled on him due to his size. But after she found her groove, he held onto her ass as she rode them both into a breathtaking climax.

Brie didn't want to assume they were in a relationship. He still had his divorce and the aftermath to deal with, and she knew he needed time to process everything. Her phone rang, and she frowned at the unknown number.

"Hello?"

"Is Brie Calhoun available?"

"Speaking. Who is calling?"

"My name is Barney Morton. I'm the location manager for Prime Prysm Studios, and I wanted to talk to you about using your hotel as a location spot for a feature movie." Brie placed a hand over her racing heart and got comfortable on the bed for their conversation.

In his hotel room, Xander took a hot shower as soon as he walked into his suite. It wasn't to get Brie's scent off him, but due to the fact it was hot as balls outside. The short walk from his vehicle to the lobby had his shirt sticking to him. He didn't linger too long because he was eager to get back to Brie. Her passion and eagerness had surprised the hell out of him, and he enjoyed it. Just thinking about her lush lips, voluptuous tits, and sweetness between her thighs made him hard again. Putting on clean clothes, his cellular chimed, and it was Starr calling. Ignoring the phone, he gathered things to put in his overnight bag, not paying attention to the phone that kept ringing. Making sure he had everything, Xander left the room and headed to the grocery store.

Having put on white cotton shorts and a matching camisole, Brie sat on the arm of the couch looking at the weather channel. The city was having a heat wave, and the temperature jumped up to a high of ninety-nine degrees without the heat index. She didn't want to admit it, but she was anxiously waiting on Xander to return to her place. She liked having him around and the time they spent together… she also wanted to get back into bed with him.

She flipped through the channels until she stopped on *First Blood*. Rambo was giving his tearful speech at the end of the movie when the doorbell rang. She opened the door for him, seeing him carrying store bags and a black overnight bag. Brie felt the heat as soon as she opened the door and she scowled.

"Dang, it's hot!" she exclaimed, quickly closing and locking the door.

"Tell me about it. I saw some people grilling pork chops on the sidewalk outside." Brie laughed, and he took his shoes off.

She put the food away and passed him a bottle of water

from the fridge. "The people from the movie studio called after you left," she informed him as she sat next to him on the couch, glancing at the screen that was now showing *Die Hard*.

"For real? What did they say?"

"They're going to fly out to meet with me and see the hotel on Tuesday."

"That's great, Brie. If they like what they see, and they use the hotel, that definitely would bring in more business."

Brie nodded at what he said, getting all hot and bothered sitting next to him. His cell phone, which he had placed on the counter, buzzed, and she looked at him. "Do you need to get that?"

He shook his head and watched as she climbed off the sofa and got down on her knees in front of him. Brie pushed his legs open further to make room for her, and she tugged at his belt. She wanted to return the oral sex kindness from last night, but they had been too occupied. Xander ran his fingers down her loose hair and threw his head back when her mouth closed over his rigid penis. It had been so long since he had gotten this type of attention, and his skin was singeing like a firecracker.

Unable to keep his eyes away from the sight, he watched in sexual wonder as Brie was attentive and hungry at the same time. His dick became shiny from her mouth and saliva while she sucked with the right amount of pressure. She didn't mind when he gripped her hair in his tight fists and controlled the slow, up-and-down motion. Her sensitive nipples brushed against her shirt, and the sensation caused her to moan, which vibrated on his penis. Xander let out a manly hiss when she floated her tongue over his testicles and gently drew them into her inviting mouth.

"Goddamn it, Brie! Open your mouth wider," he instructed when she took his stiff rod back inside her mouth. She didn't know how long she was on her knees giving Xander a blow job, but she wanted it to last, and she was very wet and ready for him. He pushed her back before he shattered, and they found themselves on the floor in front of the TV stand with Xander pounding inside her from behind. Her nails made scratch marks on the carpet from the deep thrusts, and Xander had a firm grip on her waist as he pounded deeply inside her. Skin slapped against moist flesh, causing a beat that was like music to them, and they didn't stop to consider that they were fucking without any protection.

Hours later, Brie was sitting at the counter observing Xander cook. She watched him brown the beef strips that he had cut and seasoned for the pepper steak. That last sexual episode had left them depleted of energy after they had draining orgasms and ended up falling asleep on the floor with Xander's arms wrapped around her.

"Who taught you how to cook?" Brie asked, taking a sip of wine as he diced a bell pepper.

"My mother. She didn't want me to starve in case I married a woman who couldn't cook."

"How is she doing, by the way?"

"She's doing good. Dad feels better having the EpiPen around. Thank you for asking."

She waved away his last words. "I'm glad everything worked out."

"Speaking of parents, have you heard from Theo recently?"

"We talked briefly last week. He was so excited because he had fed a baby koala bear a few days prior." They chuckled at that, and he placed the diced vegetables to the side.

"He's living the dream on that cruise, huh?"

"Yes, and I'm glad. He might want to plan another one once he gets back home." After dinner, they had snuggled on the couch and watch an eighties-movie marathon on the television. Since it was a scorching weekend and they had plenty of food and beverages in the house, they didn't have any reason to leave, and honestly, they didn't want to. Xander felt unbelievably at peace while spending time with Brie. There was no drama, no secrets, no bullshit. It was only laughs, smiles, and deep conversations. If he could, Xander would have it so the weekend would never end, but they both knew things would go back to reality in two days.

Chapter 14

It had just turned one p.m. when the people from Prime Prysm Studios left the hotel. They fell in love with Dynasty Towers and was amazed by the penthouse for the movie scene. Brie had shown them the available rooms, and they liked the third one, and she didn't say anything while they were making notes and speaking in hushed tones. It was the location manager, Barney, and three assistants with an executive producer who had shown up for the meeting and had reconvened in the conference room after they left the penthouse.

The six of them had spoken of insurance, security, compensation, layouts, and a lot of unfamiliar terms Brie wasn't sure of, and they were very patient when she asked questions. They told her a contract would be drawn up and sent in a few days after they spoke to the director and some studio bigwigs. Once she looked over it and her lawyers gave the thumbs up and if Brie signed it, there would be a non-disclosure addendum that the employees would have to sign saying they couldn't talk about what took place at the hotel nor take pictures during production.

Brie was excited about the movie shoot, not to mention the publicity it would bring to the establishment. She closed her leather-bound notebook and waited for the elevator. She tried to call Faith as soon as the meeting ended, but it went to voicemail, so she texted her friend to call her when she was free. Brie decided to call her dad when she got home to let him know about the good news and knew he'd be just as excited.

Brie was trying everything in her power not to think about Xander. Ever since he left her house on Sunday night, she couldn't stop thinking about their amazing weekend together. It wasn't just the incredible, crazy, hot sex they had that made it memorable. It was the talking and bonding they shared. He had told her about his dreams for the company, and she had discussed her goals for the hotel. They were both ambitious and could understand each other's desire to be successful.

They hadn't spoken since then, which was probably for the best since they had to give each other space and not appear too clingy. Brie walked out the elevator and headed for her office; stopping short when she saw Xander talking to Darla, and the older woman was smiling.

"Hello." She felt her skin heat up under his smoldering

232

gaze, and she took a shuddering breath. He was leaning against the wall with one hand clutching blueprints, and the other was in his pants pocket. He was wearing a midnight-blue button down with a black tie and black trousers.

"Hi. How did it go with the movie people?" Darla demanded with glee, and Brie giggled before answering her assistant, straining to keep her eyes from lingering on Xander. Darla hung onto Brie's every word, and her eyes lit up.

"That's good news," Xander added after she had finished, and she smiled. "I have news about the renovations," he said holding up the prints as she unlocked the door.

"Darla, you can go home if you want. I'm going to be on calls the rest of the day."

"Are you sure?"

"Yes, I'll clock you out for a full day." She informed the woman as Xander walked past her, and the scent of his cologne drifted in her nostrils.

"OK, thank you. I think I'll treat myself to an afternoon movie." Darla was up and away from her desk in seconds. Brie closed the door and made sure she locked it. Xander dropped the papers he held, stormed over to her and kissed her deeply

233

as he cradled her face.

Brie sighed with pleasure as they nestled into the smooch. His thumbs caressed the curve of her throat; her hands clutching his middle to bring his body closer to hers. His left hand cupped the back of her neck, and she slanted her head to keep her mouth on his. She missed this so much! Brie got excited when the kiss became more ardent and heated. Xander released her lips seconds later and moved to nibble her neck.

Her breasts became achy, and Brie wanted Xander to fondle them. The raw pulsation she had felt all weekend came back with a vengeance when she saw him a few moments ago, and she felt like her body was burning from the inside out. Xander was panting deeply, and his erection was becoming more uncomfortable with each second that passed.

"Do you realize that I have thought about nothing else but you the past two days?" Xander asked in a husky voice; his breath causing the skin at her neck to tingle.

"I can believe it. I've thought about you too," she responded, pushing him down on the sofa, his wide shoulders taking up most of the space. Traffic sounds could be heard from the open windows, and there was a coolness in the air.

Xander looked up at her with insatiable eyes as she undid the tie and snap at her waist and the dress fell open. "Oh, yeah? What were you thinking about?"

"The weekend we had. How it was nice and peaceful. The other part..." she said in a soft voice as she sat astride on his lap. Her tits were covered by a black, satin push-up bra, and she had on a black garter belt with a satin thong.

"You look fucking sexy right now, Brie." His hands began massaging her full bosom, his index fingers grazing over the material that was hiding her hard nipples. "What about the other part?" he prodded, and she smiled.

"The parts we spent on the couch, the floor, and in the bed." Brie tugged at his belt and unsnapped his pants.

"Oh! You mean the mind-blowing, spectacular sex?" Xander inquired with a hitch in his breath when her fingers closed around his hardness.

Brie nodded as she licked the skin behind his ear and gave him a hard squeeze. Xander pulled her bra down, and she sighed when he twisted her nipples between his fingers. She let out a croaky moan when he bent down and covered the tip with his open mouth. Covering his moving head with one

235

hand, she looked through heavy eyelids as he licked and played with her breasts with his lips. The dark tips disappeared in and out his mouth as he rotated between them and flicked the tight buds.

"Harder," she gasped, grinding herself against him. Brie pushed her underwear to the side, took his dick and waved it back and forth over the top of her vagina lips.

"You're doing that shit on purpose," he mumbled, grabbing her behind and moving her forward so she could slide down on his waiting penis.

Brie's dress had fallen to her elbows, and she wrapped her arms around his neck as she began to move on him. Xander couldn't stop himself from touching her; Brie's skin was so damn soft and creamy. Their grunts and moans filled the quiet room, and they took their time with each other. They didn't know when they would be together again, and Xander wanted it to be good for her. She kissed him as her body was moving up and down on him, and Xander settled back on the cushions to give her a deeper position.

During the weekend, there had been times when they had slipped up and had sex without a condom, but Brie had reassured him that she faithfully took birth control pills and that was enough for Xander. Besides, the way she was humping him now, he hadn't even thought about protection, and he liked going at it raw with her.

"You're taking all this, huh?"

Brie nodded, licking the outline of his mouth. "You were in charge a lot this weekend; I'm just returning the favor. You like it?" She stopped bouncing on him, but he was still buried inside of her, and Brie's inner muscles clutched him tightly. Xander closed his eyes and tossed his head back, and she let out a sultry smile.

"Damn, that feels amazing, Brie," he panted, holding her hips.

"I know it does. You feel so good inside me, Xander."

"Keep doing that," he ordered and used his hands on her ass to pump inside her with deep thrusts. Between her clutching and his lunges, Brie had a huge release and was still climaxing when Xander spilled his seed inside her. What just happened was 100 percent straight fucking, and they both loved it. Xander wrapped his arms around her waist, and they stayed like that for a long time to bask in the glow and to also ponder what was going on between them.

****

Three days later, Brie glanced at the clock and turned off the oven. She covered the cooked chicken wings she just finished frying for dinner to go with the macaroni and cheese and steamed vegetables. Xander was coming over, and she was looking forward to seeing him. They had talked and sent text messages but hadn't seen each other since their rendezvous in her office. Now that they had become intimate, their conversations were more personal, and they were learning things about each other like their likes and dislikes, their pet peeves, and even discussed silly things like whether ketchup belonged in the fridge or not.

She went upstairs and walked into the bathroom where she turned on the shower. Luckily, the weather was pleasant, and she had the windows open with the ceiling fans to circulate the air. Stepping into the shower, she leaned her head to wet her hair and proceeded to take a long shower.

Xander used the spare key to let himself into the house. He smelled the food when he walked in and inhaled with appreciation.

His phone rang, and he ignored it again when he saw it was Starr. They had an appointment with the lawyers the next day, and he hoped she had signed the divorce papers. He slipped off his shoes and placed his bag by the closet door. He had brought some clothes just in case he ended up spending the night. He didn't see Brie on the first floor, so he sprinted upstairs, anxious to see her. Seeing her body silhouetted through the frosted shower curtain, he took his clothes off with a deep grin.

Brie was running a hand down her wet arm when she turned her head and saw Xander slip in.

"Mind if I join you?"

She shook her head no and looked away as her heart was hammering. This was the first time she had shared a shower with a man, and it was very erotic. The space seemed smaller with him in it, and she didn't care. He stepped back to admire her backside, and he got semi-erect. Brie peeked over her shoulder, and again, their eyes met through the humid steam.

"I don't have any manly-smelling body wash," she mentioned as she turned to face him.

"I know. My soap is in my bag downstairs, but I'm not

leaving to get it. Besides, I'm willing to smell like…" He reached behind her to turn the body wash label toward them. "Cranberry Splash for you." Brie laughed at that as her fingers rested on his waist.

"This is the first shower I've taken with a man," she confessed, and he grinned.

"Good. I'm glad I was your first with this." His hands were on her wet shoulders, and he moved them down her arms.

"Natalie called me earlier. She invited me to their fight party on Saturday."

"Yeah, I'll be there too." They knew they had to go in separate cars so there wouldn't be any talk. Brie and Xander wasn't trying to hide being together, but they weren't ready for the world to know about their private business.

"Dinner is ready," she said as he moved his hands down to squeeze and rub her rear end.

"I know. I smelled the food when I walked in."

Brie placed her head on his shoulder, and he ran his hand up and down her back in small, soothing circles. "Are you OK?" he whispered, and she nodded.

"Just taking in the moment," she replied softly. He took a

profound breath; his lips resting against her forehead.

"I'm not going anywhere, Brie."

She looked up at him, running a finger down his strong jawline. "Xander—"

"Hush and let me finish, babe. You know how long I've been married. But honestly, it felt like I wasn't in a marriage. We didn't talk, didn't go out, didn't take vacations. We didn't do any of the normal things married couples do. I felt alone. I wanted the type of marriage my parents and friends have. I don't want you to think that I'm jumping from a marriage to a relationship because I'm not. But I do want to continue spending time with you, Brie. Last weekend was one of the best ones I've had in a long time, and it was because of the time spent here with you. I haven't felt that type of mental and physical closeness in years, and I don't want it to end."

Brie sniffled as tears fell down her cheeks. She used him to balance herself as she stood on her tippy toes and pressed her lips against his.

"Don't cry, babe."

"They're happy tears. I know you're going through a lot right now, but just know that I'm here for you. My door is always open, and my ear will always be available. I know you're not the type of guy to jump from one to another. I am enjoying our time as well, but I know whatever this is that we're doing, we have to take it one day at a time. I'm not pressuring you to define this or put a label on it," she reassured him while rubbing her middle with his. Xander let out a genuine smile and cupped her head as she hunched down and wrapped her lips around his waiting penis.

Simultaneously, Starr snorted another line of cocaine and sat back to let the drugs take effect. She was at Casey's house, and the same thing was going on that they were used to. It was a lot of people there, and it was a lot going on. Casey had a huge bedroom, and there were a total of eight people occupying it. Some were on the settee talking and laughing, while others ate from the pizza boxes that were stacked on a table in the corner, and others were having sex. Starr didn't know any of them, but with the endless supply of weed and coke being passed around the room, she was in heaven.

She had tried the drug the day after she got the divorce papers, and she fucking loved it! She made it a point to get high whenever she could, and Casey seemed to know where to get the best brand from. Starr still couldn't believe that Xander was trying to divorce her. She hadn't signed the papers and didn't plan on doing it. She thought about lying and saying she was pregnant but decided against it since it had been almost a year since she had slept with her husband. She didn't know what would happen at the meeting with the lawyers, but she knew she was going to pull every trick in the book to keep Xander. She was reclining on a settee wearing only a silk robe when a black guy with braids walked over to her and motioned for her to turn around. She felt lethargic yet gratified when the man inserted himself inside her ass without a condom.

****

Mr. Seamus looked at his Rolex, noting there were five minutes left before the mediation got underway. Starr and her lawyer had yet to arrive, and he looked at Xander who was staring out the window. The younger man was wearing a gray suit with a black shirt, and Glenn knew Xander didn't want to be here.

"You look pensive. Having a change of heart?" Glenn asked, and he looked at his lawyer sharply.

"Hell no! I'm thinking about something else." It was more

like someone else.

Xander's mind was on Brie, and he was counting down the minutes until he saw her again. The meeting was to take place in one of the conference rooms at Glenn's firm, and Xander hoped it wouldn't take all day to get this done. There was a knock on the door, and Starr was shown in with her attorney. She had on an ivory suit with her hair slicked back. Her lawyer was an older white woman with thinning, brown hair.

"Good morning. Would either of you like some coffee?" Glenn offered. They declined, and the four people sat down at the circular, glass table. Starr stared at her husband, hoping he would look at her, but Xander wasn't paying her any attention.

"This is an agreed upon settlement meeting between both Sterling parties, and hopefully, we can come to a resolution. I have here a signed certified mail receipt that the divorce papers were delivered. Did you receive them, Mrs. Sterling?" Glenn began the meeting, and he uncapped his gold pen while waiting on Starr to answer.

"Yes, they were received. My client does not want the divorce and will not sign the papers," Margaret Keys spoke up, and Xander looked angrily at Starr.

"Is there any reason why you are prolonging this?"

She let out a deep breath and closed her eyes while placing a hand over her heart. Xander rolled his eyes because he knew she was being melodramatic and putting on a show for the other two people in the room.

"I love you, Xander. I always have. I want to work on our relationship."

"We're way past that point. Just sign the papers, and we can go on with our separate lives."

"No. I'll try anything, Xander. We can try counseling again. What about group meetings? We can even go see a pastor."

"Starr, stop it! I'm not backtracking when we could've tried those things before now. I'm not staying with a cheater. I'll file uncontested if I have to."

"OK, let's all calm down. Mr. Sterling, my client wants you to understand the full situation, and once you do, see if you'll have a change of heart," Ms. Keys stated, opening up her leather briefcase.

"What are you talking about?"

"A few years ago, my client saw a doctor; a specialist to be exact. During those sessions, my client was diagnosed with a sexual addiction. I have here a signed affidavit from said doctor confirming it." Margaret slid the paper to Glenn who read over it, while Xander glared at her.

"You are so full of it, Starr. We've been together since college. I didn't know anything about those doctor's visits. You could've come to me about this at any time. Why say something now?"

Starr looked at her lawyer, who patted her arm. "I didn't tell you because I was ashamed. I didn't know how to tell you."

"And that gives you a pass to go out and cheat on me? I wouldn't be surprised if that was what you were doing when you came home late all those times. You were out fucking around on me!"

Glenn patted his back as he looked up from the form. "Did you just graduate from law school, Ms. Keys?" Xander's lawyer asked, putting the paper down.

"Excuse me? I went to Princeton, graduated at the top of my class and—"

"And you know this is inadmissible in court. First, this is hearsay, and there's that whole doctor-patient confidentiality clause."

"Look, Mr. Seamus, I—"

"But it's the truth!" Starr interrupted, moving closer to the edge of the chair. She thought once Xander heard the news, he would call the whole thing off, and they would walk out the office together. *He's supposed to understand!*

"Mrs. Sterling, we have that incriminating video, and you have no prenuptial agreement. My client has agreed to let you keep the house. Of course, he'll take his name off the mortgage and bills. Also—"

"You know I don't have the money to keep up the house, Xander," she said matter-of-factly, and he shrugged.

"Then sell it. I don't care."

"Why are you being so mean to me?"

He shook his head and ran his hand down his face. "The deal won't get any better than this. Sign the papers, Starr."

"No. I'm going to fight for us!"

"There is no point. I'm not in love with you anymore; I haven't felt any love for you in a long time."

Starr's eyes got big at that proclamation, and her heart felt like it was breaking. It wasn't what she wanted to hear and didn't know he had felt that way. *Xander doesn't love me anymore!* She got her purse and ran out the office without speaking to Margaret. She mumbled that she would get in touch with Glenn in a few days and followed her client out the room.

"She is unbelievable!" Xander barked as he stood up and yanked at his tie. A sex addict? What in the hell was Starr trying to do?

"Be that as it may, you can't file an uncontested divorce. She has to sign the documents, Xander."

"She's just going to draw this out."

"Are you offering any other incentives?" his lawyer asked gently.

"I'm not paying spousal support if that's what you're asking. Not after what she did. All I'm offering is the house." Glenn nodded and stood up as well. "I'll call you after I hear from her lawyer." Xander nodded and left the office after the two shook hands.

****

The rest of the week passed by uneventful. He hadn't been back to Brie's house because he needed to clear his head after the mediation, but he did text her. Starr had sent him several messages, but Xander didn't reply to them. He didn't have anything to say and was pissed she wasn't moving forward with things.

It was the night of the fight party, and he left the hotel room to head for Marshall's house in Oak Park. He was looking forward to hanging out with some friends and seeing Brie. That put him in a better mood as he steered his truck into the weekend traffic. At Natalie and Marshall's house, Brie looked around at the people talking in the living and dining room. There were sixteen people in all, and she smiled when her friend strutted over to her.

"You know you love throwing parties," Brie told Natalie, and she giggled. They were standing in the kitchen as people were walking around and eating while waiting on the fight to start. The big-screen TV was showing the pre-show, and the dining room had a buffet of finger foods, desserts, and cocktails.

"Girl, this time it was Marshall's doing. Thanks for

coming."

"Thank you for the invite." Brie wore a white halter dress and had a pink flower in her hair.

"You're welcome. A lot of women usually don't come, so I'll have someone to talk to," Natalie let her know as the doorbell rang.

Out of all the guests, including Brie and Natalie, there were only two other women there with their husbands. Xander walked in, and his frat brothers greeted him loudly. Brie's pulse increased at the sight of him, and she pressed her lips together, watching him walk to the cooler to empty the case of beer he bought with him.

"Plus, I told Marshall to invite some nice, single guys for you to meet," Natalie said with a crafty grin.

"You did what?" Brie was eating some grapes from the fruit tray, and she looked at the other woman with big eyes.

"Don't be mad, Brie. You're pretty, and his friends are cool. Trust me."

Brie sipped from her lime spritzer, growing with anxiety over Natalie's words. She wasn't looking to date someone right now. It had nothing to do with the fact that she was involved with Xander, but she just didn't want to be in a relationship right now. Xander walked into the kitchen and kissed the hostess on the cheek.

"Hello, ladies."

"Hi, Xander," Brie said softly, seeing the craving in his eyes.

"Let's get Xander's opinion," Natalie chimed in, unaware of the looks between the adults.

"On what?" he asked, pulling his gaze from Brie.

"I was telling her that I told my hubby to invite some of his available friends so she could meet them. Don't you think someone should snatch her up? She's a good catch, right?"

You don't know the half of it, he thought. "She's more than that. These dudes aren't worthy of her." Xander strolled away after that, and Brie thought her heart was going to burst out her chest at his words. Natalie walked away as well, and Brie licked her lips and inwardly smiled, closing her eyes for a second.

Brie went to the buffet table, and Xander was putting boneless wings on a paper plate. They were the only two at the table, and Brie looked around, noticing no one was paying them any attention.

"Hey."

"Hey."

"You look nice tonight," she mentioned, taking in his jeans and black shirt.

"Thanks, so do you. That's a pretty dress." She grinned, pushing her hair behind her ear.

"So Natalie is trying to set you up, huh?" he asked, reaching for the salad.

"I didn't know anything about that," she quickly replied as she played with a napkin.

"Yeah, I figured. She likes to set people up on blind dates," Xander retorted in a deep voice. The guests got excited as the announcers started listing the boxers' stats.

"Go for a ride with me later," Xander said, turning to face her. To the other people in the house, it looked like they were making small talk, but it was more than that to them. Brie nodded and looked him up and down before walking away; Xander watching her saunter away with an amused grin.

The fight started a few minutes later, and it lasted for seven rounds. As the winner was being interviewed, the women congregated in the dining room. Xander was standing in a circle with his buddies, and they were talking about the short fight. From where he stood, he could see Brie laughing and talking. She turned her head when she felt his eyes on her and smiled at him with caring eyes. They ended up staying for two hours, and Xander followed Brie back to the city.

She parked her car and rushed to his truck as rain began to fall. Xander headed toward the lake on 53rd Street while he turned on the windshield wipers at full speed against the rapidly falling water. He got to the end of the road and turned left into a parking lot of one of the high-rise condominiums. He found a space at the end and parked the vehicle. Brie hummed along to Xander's slow jams CD as she unbuckled her seat belt and set her purse at her feet.

"Did you bet on the fight?" she asked, turning her body in his direction.

"Thankfully, no. Did you have fun?"

"I had a good time. You?" Xander nodded, turning the wipers off with the car before he unsnapped his safety belt as well.

"Thank you for what you said to Natalie."

"It was the truth," he replied right away, and she felt giddy inside.

"How have you been?" Brie wondered, seeing the muscles pressed against his shirt. He gave her the edited version of the meeting with the lawyers, and she took a deep breath.

"I'm sorry, Xander." She exhaled, watching him look out the window, knowing he was in deep thought. Brie didn't know what else to say regarding the situation. All she could do was listen as he vented.

"Maybe her attorney can talk some sense into Starr," she suggested in a soothing tone.

"Hopefully," Xander mumbled. "Thank you for listening."

"You're welcome. Whenever you need to talk, I'm here." Brie reminded him as he grabbed her hand, his thumb rubbing over her knuckles.

"How was your week?" he asked, the inside of the truck vibrating from his deep, booming voice.

"It was crazy. Two people who went for the random drug tests reported positive results, and I had to fire them. So I've been dealing with that and interviewing people," she answered, noting he was paying attention to what she was saying.

"Any luck with the candidates?" She shook her head, interlocking their hands.

Xander was looking at her like he wanted to eat her alive, and it was doing something to her. Her skin started to prickle with sexual quivers, and she licked her lips before she leaned toward him. She went for his cheek, but before she could move away, Xander cupped the back of her head to push his lips on hers. The truck had been custom made, so the driver's seat was a few inches wider than usual, and when he pulled her over to straddle him, her knees were resting comfortably against his thighs. Xander lowered his seat so that it was on an angle, and her hands rested on his chest.

"Comfy?" she asked with a smile and he nodded. "It's a good thing your windows are tinted."

"You can say that again." Brie slowly bent down to Xander, their lips grazing each other. She took the tip of her tongue and traced his top lip, then the bottom one.

"Mmmm, I like that," he announced, and she grinned again before kissing him. It was slow, and there was a lot of tongue involved. Her tongue had a fruity taste to it, and she laughed in her throat when he suckled on it. His hands moved down her back to grasp her round butt where he caressed and massaged her plump booty. Brie briefly closed her eyes as she felt him move his hands under her dress toward her center; his middle finger skimming the outer lips through her underwear.

"Uh huh, you're not wet enough yet," he stated against her swollen lips. Brie moved up and shifted against his fingers. She slid her hands between their bodies to undo his belt. Reaching inside his jeans, she began fondling his hard length, and he cursed under his breath.

"What are you going to do about it?"

"Give me about five minutes," he retorted, pushing the top of her dress down. The radio automatically cut off, and with the sounds of the heavy rain, the truck was filled with Brie's soft moans and Xander's masculine noises. Her dress had a built-in bra, so when he tugged her outfit down, her breasts popped out and brushed alongside his chest.

She sighed with fulfilment when he wrapped his lips around her left nipple and pulled it into his waiting mouth. While Xander was rotating between her well-endowed tits, she fully undid his pants and pulled out his erect penis. The tip was wet, and she ran her thumb over the opening. Brie was ready for him, and he shifted her higher when she guided him inside her soaked wetness after pushing her panties to the side.

Bracing herself on his chest, she slowly rode him up and down. Xander loved seeing her consumed in passion. He didn't mind if she rode him fast or slow, just as long as he was able to stay buried deep inside her. Xander caressed her bottom lip with his thumb, and she drew it into her mouth. Long, bountiful thrusts later, Brie had a huge climax. Her whimpers were like music to his ears. He grabbed her tushy and continued to move her on him, causing her to have another release as he spilled a big load inside her.

Chapter 15

Starr eyed the lobby of Dynasty Towers and was surprised at how elegant it looked. She headed toward the elevators with one goal in mind: to kick Brie Calhoun's ass. After that nightmare of a meeting with the attorneys and Xander saying he didn't love her anymore, she had hired a private investigator to follow him around with a loan she had gotten from Casey. It had taken a few days, but from the report, one thing was evident: Xander was spending nights at Brie's house.

The visits had happened every few days, but she knew they were fucking around. Of course, she didn't have any proof since the pictures only showed him entering and leaving at various times, but she felt it in her heart. The PI was able to tell her Brie's full name, where she worked, and who she was. Starr couldn't believe the nerdy girl who had tutored Xander in school was the one he was spending all his time with. Xander still wasn't taking her calls, and she bet it was because of Brie.

"Hello. Can I help you?" Darla asked, looking at Starr over her spectacles when the woman walked through the outer glass door.

"Tell your boss that Mrs. Xander Sterling would like a word with her," Starr proclaimed with an attitude, clutching her Gucci purse.

"Do you have an appointment?"

"No, I do not."

She looked at Starr again and picked up the phone. After a few words with Darla, Brie put the phone down and wondered why Starr was here. She wasn't scared of the unscheduled visit, but she was curious. She had told Darla to let five minutes pass before allowing Starr to enter. Brie stood up and went to lean against the front of her desk. She was wearing an orange business dress with heels. Starr barged in without knocking and left the door open.

"Can I help you, Starr? Brie asked, getting right to the point.

"What does he see in you?" Starr questioned incredulously with disgust.

"Excuse me?"

"I asked, what does my husband see in you?"

Brie's eyebrows went up at the query. "Is that why you're

259

here?"

"I'm here to tell you to stay away from Xander. He's still my husband." Brie let out a deep breath, realizing that Starr had hit the nail on the head with her statement. She knew they were separated and had been for weeks, but they technically were still married.

"OK, Starr. I'm not going to argue with you."

"I'm not arguing either. I'm just stating a fact."

Brie got irritated by that and Starr's demeanor; like she had a right to be here. "First of all, this is my place of business, and you won't disrespect that. Second, I don't know how you're claiming a man who is divorcing you."

Starr dashed over to Brie with anger on her face. Who in the hell was Brie to talk to her like this?

"You don't know what the fuck you're talking about!" Starr reached out to poke Brie in her chest, but before Starr could blink, Brie had taken her wrist, twisted it, and caused Starr to drop on her knees, and Brie applied pressure to the back of her elbow. Getting bad vibes from Starr, Darla had called security when she went inside the office. The guards walked in just in time to see Starr approach Brie and their employer defend herself.

"Call the police!" both women shouted. One officer stepped between the women, and as soon as Brie let Starr go, she started cursing and yelling, trying to fight her.

This is not worth it, Brie mused. Minutes later, the police had arrived, and they had jumped in to calm Starr down. They ended up getting statements, and the officers suggested that Brie get a restraining order after bellowing at Starr who wouldn't shut up. After Starr was escorted off the property and told not to come back, she headed next door to the construction site.

After taking the stairs and shouting for Xander, she found him on the eighth floor talking to Marshall. The latter nudged Xander, and he looked up to see his pissed off wife. He groaned and went to meet her before she could make a scene. Before he could say anything, she hit his chest and went off on him.

"You tell that bitch she's going to hear from my lawyer!"

"What the hell are you talking about?" Xander questioned, grabbing her arm and pulling her to a corner.

"I went to confront your girlfriend, and she put her hands

on me. You tell her that was the biggest mistake she ever made!"

Xander closed his eyes to control his fury, and the only thing he thought about was seeing Brie and making sure she was okay. He didn't believe Starr's story; as he knew she tended to exaggerate.

"Leave, Starr," he said simply, and she looked at him with disbelief.

"Aren't you going to ask about my well-being, Xander? She attacked me!"

"No. If Brie did touch you, you probably started it."

"I can't believe you're taking her side. I'm your wife."

Xander left her standing there and walked out the building. Brie was leaning against the window, looking at the lake. She could see people swimming, sailing, and the buoys were bouncing from the small waves. She was glad Qyle had made her take those self-defense classes at the YMCA since they came in handy today. She wasn't looking for those skills to come out, but she wasn't going to let Starr put her hands on her either. She was going to do what the police officers suggested and get a restraining order in the morning since she didn't want a repeat altercation to happen in the future. There was a hard knock on the door, and she turned to see Xander walk in.

"Are you all right, Brie?" he asked as he advanced on her, and she backed away from him. The movement wasn't lost to Xander, and she nodded.

"Yes, I'm fine. But your crazy ass wife needs to stay away from me. This is my office, and I'm not dealing with that here."

"I'm sorry about her behavior. What happened?" Brie replayed the last few moments in her office, and his hands tightened into fists. "Are you sure you're OK?"

"Yep," she replied with her arms folded across her chest.

"I have a feeling that's not true."

Brie rubbed the back of her head and sighed. "Xander, I'm not used to this. Disgruntled wives barging into my office, making demands, and then want to fight me. This is drama, and I don't like drama." She informed him, sitting on the arm of the couch.

"I know, Brie—"

"Do you?"

"What the hell does that mean?"

"You don't know if this will happen again or not."

"Brie—"

She held up her hand, and he stopped talking. "We should take a step back from each other, just until the smoke clears."

"I don't want that, and you're letting Starr stop us from-"

"I don't want her to use our relationship to hurt you. She could go to the media, and it'll be your name and reputation on the line since you two are still married."

"Through no fault of mine!" Xander barked.

"I know."

"I don't get a say in this?"

Brie bit her bottom lip, her eyes drilling into his. It took everything in her not to burst out crying. Of course she didn't want to stop seeing Xander, but this put a lot of things into perspective for her.

"I'm not saying we'll never talk to each other again. I just… we have to cool things down a bit." Brie closed her eyes and a lone tear ran down her cheek when he left the office and slammed the door after him.

****

The next night, Xander pulled up in the driveway of his old house behind a Lexus that he didn't recognize. He looked around and noticed it was the only house on the block with an unkempt lawn. He used to tend to the outside of the house on a weekly basis, and it seemed like Starr stopped caring how it looked. He used the spare key to let himself in, and he recoiled from the stench in the air. The house was stale, and there seemed to be no ventilation.

The dining room table had been set for two, but there weren't any people on the first level. Xander headed upstairs, and as soon as he got to the landing, he heard grunts coming from the bedroom. He pulled out his phone and started to record what he came across. The last time he had done so, he had benefitted from it, and he might get lucky again. The dresser was by the door, and the first thing he saw was an open package of heroin and half of it was gone. Looking toward the bed, Xander saw a husky white man behind Starr, drilling into her like a jackhammer.

"Having fun?" Xander asked, causing the man to jump back as his small penis went limp. Starr looked at him, her eyes were glazed over, and Xander shook his head in disgust.

"Xander, honey, you came back home," she said in a somnolent voice like she was sleepy, and he knew she was high.

"Hey, you're Xander Sterling! Oh my God, I'm such a big fan!" the naked man exclaimed, walking toward Xander with his hand out to be shaken. He stopped moving at the look Xander gave him and shut his mouth.

"Al is a big fan."

"Starr, what's this? You're a drug addict now?" She chuckled as she sat up, not ashamed that she was displaying her bare body to her husband and lover at the same time.

"No, baby. I just do it every now and then. It's no big deal," she responded as her body was swaying.

"You're pathetic. Sign the divorce papers or I'm going to the police about this," Xander motioned to the drugs and walked out the room. Al went over to Starr and pushed her back on the bed. He thrusted her head toward his soft dick, and she took it in her mouth to get him hard again.

"Don't worry, babe. You can divorce him. I'll take care of you," Al told her with a hitched breath at what she was doing.

"You promise?" she asked around the flesh in her mouth.

"Yeah, sure." *As long as you get that football alimony money*, Al said to himself as he patted her cheek to egg her on.

****

Three weeks later, Brie was out shopping with Natalie, who was looking for an outfit. Her anniversary was coming up with Marshall, and she wanted to find something special for the planned outing. They were in Neiman Marcus, and Brie was sitting in the chair area next to the fitting rooms while Natalie tried on some dresses. Brie had talked to Qyle earlier that day, and she had planned a weekend getaway with her girlfriend. Qyle had told Brie they would make arrangements for her girlfriend to meet Brie once they came back.

Ever since she had told Xander that they should spend time apart, she had worked nonstop at the hotel. She had worked on Saturdays and Sundays and even offered to work on Elmo's weekend because she didn't want to be at home to let her mind wander toward Xander. She acknowledged that she missed him, and every day she wondered what he was doing. Brie had been careful to avoid running into him at the hotel by entering and exiting the building from the side kitchen entrance.

Xander probably didn't want to hear from her, and she

couldn't blame him if he felt that way. Brie was wearing a red camisole with a floor length red peasant skirt plastered with beads and sequins. It was a beautiful afternoon, and it was the first week in September. Brie was glad to be out shopping with Natalie, even though her friend had to practically drag her from the hotel. Natalie walked out of the dressing room wearing a short, silver cocktail dress.

"That's pretty. I love that color on you," Brie mentioned as she sat back on her hands.

"Yeah, I like it too," she mumbled, looking at herself in the three-way mirror. After a few more changes, Natalie ended up getting the first one with matching shoes. They headed toward the food court, and they shared an order of nachos. Natalie ate a chip and eyed Brie. She was here, but she wasn't here. Natalie had a good idea where Brie's head was at, but she'd feel her out first.

"Where is Marshall taking you for your anniversary?" Brie inquired, looking around the semi-full eating area. Because it was a weekday, the mall wasn't packed, and they were able to go from store to store without a bunch of crowds.

"I don't know. He's being extra secretive about it. Are you

OK, Brie?"

She finished chewing her food before responding. "I'm fine. Why do you ask?"

"You seem a little distracted," Natalie voiced honestly.

Brie sighed, sitting back in the plastic chair. "I have been a little bit. I'm sorry for being a bad shopping companion."

"It's fine. Do you want to talk about anything?"

Brie realized she should talk to her friend and get some opinions on the situation. "Xander and I have been spending a lot of time together. Starr caused an argument, and I told him we should take some time apart. I miss him, Natalie."

"I'm not surprised by what you told me. I saw the looks between you and him whenever we all got together. Honestly, I'm glad it finally happened. You two are good for each other. But if you miss him, why not call?"

"He doesn't want to talk to me, and he's probably still mad."

"He might not be. You never know."

"Even if he's not, Xander is still married, and Starr isn't going to change that anytime soon."

Natalie knew of the updated situation regarding Xander's

marriage, but it wasn't her place to say anything. "You should call him. He's probably feeling the same way you are. Better yet, go see him."

Brie bit her lip and let out a deep breath. She did want to see and talk to Xander; even if it was to make sure he was doing okay. "He's most likely still at work now," Brie professed, looking at her watch.

"Oh, he's not there. Marshall said he's been working consistently for weeks, and he made Xander take a few days off."

"OK, I'll go. I'll see you later."

"Good luck, girl." Brie nodded, picked up her shopping bags, and left the mall in a hurry.

****

In his hotel room, Xander was sitting at the table going through the home listings his realtor had emailed him. The home seller had shown Xander several houses in different parts of the city, but none seemed right. He had on a gray tank top and gray basketball shorts. After working back-to-back the past few weeks and going to see houses in between, he was exhausted and wanted to chill for the next few days.

Being busy had kept his mind off Brie during the day, even though the thoughts of her didn't stop at night. He resisted calling her because he didn't want to bother her or get on her nerves. He didn't blame her for distancing himself after what Starr had done. It was pointless, and Starr was wrong for what she did. Xander honestly wished he could've stopped it from occurring, but maybe it happened for a reason. It allowed them to take a step back and re-evaluate their feelings for each other.

There was a soft knock on the door, and he glanced at the clock next to the bed. He had ordered a Giordano's pizza thirty minutes ago and was told it would be an hour before it was delivered. Xander opened the door and was surprised to see Brie standing on the other side. He leaned against the door; his right arm resting on the jam above his head. Brie's heart was beating so fast as she expected him to shut the door in her face.

"Hi," she said after clearing her throat.

"Hey," he replied in an indifferent tone.

"Can I come in?" Brie was silent as Xander slowly looked her up and down, sizing her up. She had to confess that her body grew hot at the look, and she mentally screamed at herself to focus. Xander stepped back and opened it wider to allow her to enter. Brie strolled into the bright room and was hit with the cold air from the air conditioner. The hotel entrepreneur in her appreciated the big, spacious room, and she looked around the suite. She stood next to the cream-colored couch as he leaned against the table with his arms crossed.

"Am I keeping you from anything?" she asked him, breaking the ice.

"It can wait."

"How have you been, Xander?"

"Busy. You?"

"Working a lot."

"What do you want, Brie?" he questioned. He hadn't said it with an attitude, but he wanted to know why she was here, and she pressed her lips together before answering.

"I came to see how you were doing, Xander, and to tell you that I really miss you. I realize that I'm the last person you want to see after I said some things you didn't want to hear, but I just wanted to make sure you were OK. Sorry I barged in like this." Brie let everything tumble out at once and then left the room after her declaration. Xander didn't move as he processed her words, not expecting her to say what she said.

Go after her! a voice inside his head screamed. Xander rushed to the door and yanked it open. He looked down the hall and saw Brie leaning against the wall with her head bent down inches from the hotel door. Xander grabbed her around her waist and pulled her back inside the room. He was rough as he pressed her up against the wall, and their lips attacked one another. Their hands were all over each other; grabbing, scratching, stroking, and caressing.

The kiss was intense and thorough, Xander trapped her wrists in one hand above her head as the other one ran down her face and her chest and continued until he yanked her skirt down. He harshly picked her up as Brie's hands went to his face and back, her nails scraping down his back. Xander reached inside his shorts, pulled out his hard dick, and Brie moaned as he slipped inside her.

It turned into minutes of hardcore, raw fucking against the entryway. She had her legs tightly wrapped around his middle that gradually loosened with each thrust. Xander lifted her left leg to provide more force, and she gently bit his earlobe. After a satisfying climax from both people, he enfolded one arm around her as he walked them to the bed across the room. Brie still had on her top and matching thong when Xander dropped her ungraciously on the mattress.

She pushed her hair from her eyes as he quickly took his clothes off. Licking her lips with greedy intent, she crawled across the king-size bed and lowered her head to take him in her mouth. Xander cupped her bobbing head and looked at her as she took in his hard phallus. Brie was using her hands to stroke him as she sucked his dick. His grunts of pleasure made her horny, and she felt that welcoming pounding between her legs.

Xander's words of "keep going" and "don't stop" fueled her to keep at it and she was enjoying bringing him to extreme pleasure. Grabbing her hair, he let out a guttural curse when she flicked his balls with her tongue. He sat down on the bed and pulled Brie to her feet and turned her around so her back was to his chest, and she eased down on his glistening cock. Xander reached around to cup her breasts over her shirt while she braced her hands on his knees and started to move up and down.

Brie closed her eyes and delighted in the feeling of him moving in and out her flesh. Sex hadn't been on her mind when she came to make amends, but she did miss having intercourse with him. Xander was a good lover, and he always made sure she was fulfilled at the end. He fingered her covered nipples and held onto her hips as she continued bouncing on him. Time went by unnoticed as Brie had two creamy orgasms, and Xander had his forehead resting on her back after he came. There was a quick knock on the door, and neither moved to answer it until it sounded again.

"Pizza delivery."

"Damn, I forgot about that," Xander mumbled as he flopped back on the bed.

"I'll get it," Brie panted as she stood up on wobbly legs. She put her skirt back on, grabbed the money off the coffee table and answered the door. Seconds later, she appeared with a medium box and placed it on the dresser. Xander motioned for her to come to him, and she obliged him after shimmying out of her skirt. Brie climbed in the bed and leaned over Xander to connect her lips to his as he lifted her shirt over her head.

****

Hours later, they were laying against the headboard with the pizza box sitting between them. Brie was wearing his shirt, and Xander was naked.

"I haven't had Giordano's in forever," Brie commented after eating three slices.

Xander nodded while looking at her. He was so glad Brie was here. He felt a lot better now that they had talked. It wasn't just the amazing sex, but it was just the fact that she was here with him.

"You want some more?"

"No, I'm full." Brie reached for the water bottle that Xander was holding, and she took a sip. When they finally got to the pizza, it was cold, but they still ate it.

"Are you going to work tomorrow?" Brie asked as she leaned back on some pillows.

"No, not until Monday. I been off this whole week. What about you?"

"The same thing. Elmo and Darla banned me from the hotel until next week."

"Looks like we have a few days together. What shall we do?"

"Well, since you're not going to let me go home to get some clothes, I—"

"Oh, you're not going anywhere." He interrupted.

Brie smiled at that. "You're fine with me wearing this shirt for the next few days?"

"You can walk around butt ass naked, and it won't bother me," Xander reassured her, and she giggled.

"I bet it won't," she responded in a low voice.

"As you can see, I have no problem with the naked form."

"Oh, I've noticed," Brie replied as her eyes ran up and down his body. Xander got up and placed the box on the coffee table. As they were sharing a pillow, Brie reached up and cupped his cheek.

"I really did miss you, Xander," she let him know in a soft voice, and she ran her thumb over his jaw.

"What did you miss about me?" he asked her, curving his hand around her hip to draw her closer to him.

"Our conversations, you making me laugh, us hanging out." She disclosed, looking in his dark eyes.

"I wanted to call you, but I didn't want to scare you off," Xander admitted, and she squeezed her lips together.

"I wanted to call you too. I thought you were mad at me."

"I was at first, babe, but I understand why you did what you did." Brie leaned forward and placed her lips on his. They slowly kissed with a small tilt to their heads; the smell of pizza between them.

Xander pulled back and pushed Brie's hair away from her face. "Starr signed the papers two weeks ago," he spoke, and she was stunned by what he said.

"Really? What finally made her do it?"

"Apparently, she's going to get married again," he answered, rubbing his hand up and down her back. Brie made a face at that, wondering who would marry a cheater like Starr.

"How do you feel about that?"

"I'm relieved she finally did it. She's not my concern anymore."

"Did you tell your parents?"

"Yes, I did. My mom was very happy, even though she wouldn't say it." Brie was quiet as she let his words sink in. She was happy for Xander's sake but wondered where that left them. Did he want more right now? Less? She knew he wasn't going to jump back into another marriage right now, and Brie wasn't ready for that either.

"Speaking of my parents, I want you to come with me to Sunday dinner at their house," he told her out the blue, and she moved her head back to look at him.

"Xander, I don't know. I—"

"Before you say anything, it's not what you think. I just want you to come as a friend. I don't want you to think it's a meet-my-parents type of moment."

"But I am meeting your parents." She countered in a bland voice, and Xander laughed.

"You're special to me, Brie, and I want you to officially meet them." She licked her lips and let out a small puff of air. She didn't see the harm in meeting The Sterlings, just as long as it was a friendly agenda. She wasn't ready to tell Xander that she had fallen in love with him yet.

"Sure, I'll go with you. It should be fun."

"Good. Now, let's talk about you walking around naked for the rest of the day."

Chapter 16

Five days later, Xander was in his office catching up on paperwork. He had received an email from one of the Naperville project managers. They were interested in commissioning S&T for an outlet mall, and Xander put a reminder in his calendar to call back first thing in the morning. It was going on nine p.m., and he was the only one left in the office. He didn't mind staying late after being off for a few days.

He wished he could've spent more time with Brie, but they both had to get back to work. Just thinking about her made him smile. Dinner at his parents' house turned out to be a fun evening that ended with Lola, Xen, and Xander teaching Brie how to play bid whist. He remembered the conversation he had with his mother as he helped her prepare dessert after a fulfilling meal of grilled steaks, baked potatoes, and steamed asparagus.

"I like Brie," Lola told her son as he was uncovering the cherry pie.

"Good."

"You know she's in love with you, right?" Xander gave

her a peculiar look, and her eyebrows shot up at his facial expression.

"What? That's crazy, Ma. We're just friends."

"If you say so, but anyone with eyes can see it when you both look at each other."

"You both? Why are you including me?" Xander asked, leaning against the counter.

"Because you love her too, but don't know it. I can understand your reluctance after what you just went through with that ex-wife of yours."

"Whoa! Mom, you're totally wrong about this."

Xander frowned when she chuckled. "OK. You're right, honey. I'm wrong about it." He didn't like her tone or the sly grin she wasn't trying to hide.

Xander sat back in his chair to stretch, and his mother's words crept under his skin. He didn't love Brie. Yes, she was beautiful, funny, loyal, successful, and sexy as hell, but that didn't mean he was head over heels in love with her. Besides, he was a newly-divorced man and wanted to embrace life as a bachelor. His cell phone went off, and he saw Brie's name appear on the caller ID.

"Hello?"

Brie smiled at his voice. "Hey, you. What are you up to?"

"Still at the office, catching up on some things. What are you doing?"

"Oh, nothing much." Brie was sitting in her car in front of Xander's office building. She had showered and changed into a zippered dress before leaving her house.

"How was it at the hotel today?"

"It was fine; had a conference come in today. Did you eat yet?"

Xander beamed at that question. "Yes, I had a sandwich and salad a few hours ago."

"How long will you be at the office?"

"I'm leaving within the next twenty minutes. What's going on? You need something?"

You bet your ass I do! "No, I was just asking."

"Uh huh, you asked for a reason."

Brie chuckled. "I was just wondering if I came by your hotel room, what time should I leave my house to meet you there?"

"You can leave now. I'll meet you in the lobby." Xander

shut down his computer and scooped up his keys. He turned off the lights in his office and headed toward the elevator. When the bay doors opened, Xander's face lit up when he saw Brie at the back of the car. Her purse had been placed on the floor, and he watched with excited eyes as she unzipped her dress to reveal a purple push-up bra and thong.

Xander calmly approached her, dropped his bag, grasped her face, then kissed her. The elevator doors closed and made its way down. They were so consumed in their kiss to realize that it arrived on the first floor, and the doors remained open. He looped his hand around her waist and pulled her against his body. The elevator became filled with Brie's moans, and their kissing noises as her hands searched for his belt.

He turned her around so her chest was to the wall, and he lowered his head to inhale the skin at the back of her neck through her hair. Brie closed her eyes and exhaled with pleasure when he licked her neck. She felt his warm hands cup her hefty breasts and gently caress them. He absolutely loved the color against her skin, and it made him extra hard. She glided her hand around his head from behind, a soft pant escaping her submissive lips.

Brie purred like a satisfied kitten in her throat as Xander toyed with her nipples over the silky material of her bra. She loved the way he was touching her and how he seemed to know all her erogenous areas. She covered his hands with hers and felt him playing with her flesh. Tossing her head back on his shoulder, she moaned when his right hand slipped down her stomach and fumbled inside her underwear to stroke her private part. The hair felt soft against his palm, and Brie exhaled with pleasure when he stuck two fingers inside her moist heat.

Pressing his erection against her behind, Xander stroked her body while making sure to keep moving his digits in and out her middle. Brie inhaled and exhaled to match his hand thrusts, which caused her to sag along the wall.

"You make me so wet, Xander," she moaned, moving her hips back and forward.

"I can't get enough of you, Brie." Xander unfastened his trousers with one hand and shoved them down his thighs.

Brie was pushed to her tip toes to accommodate him so that he could enter her. He held her wrists together on the wall and held onto her hips as he pounded inside her with deep, meaningful movements. Brie had never had sex in an elevator before, and it was turning her on in more ways than one.

"God, I could fuck you all day." Xander panted as he placed his head against hers, his teeth scraping the shell of her ear.

"I want you to, baby."

Xander knew every time he rode this elevator, he would think about this moment when they had sex without a care in the world. He would never forget how her bare tit felt in his hand and how snug she felt around him. Her back was arched as she bounced back to match his lunges, and she liked how Xander practically lifted her off the floor so they could continue this uninhibited sexual romp.

****

Weeks later, Xander closed on a three-bedroom house in New Lenox. It was within his price range, and he liked how it wasn't too big, but it had enough space to be comfortable. As far as the renovations for the hotel, the second tower had grown to the same height as the original building, and they were now working on the frame. On the lower floors, the plumbers, electricians, and carpenters were busy erecting walls, installing wires, and pipes for the plumbing system.

A city inspector had made an impromptu visit and found everything in order and up to code. Brie knew the second tower wouldn't be ready for guest until next year, which was fine with her. She didn't want S&T to rush the job but did want most of it done before the cold weather arrived. Xander had called to follow up on the outlet mall job, and they ended up winning the bid. The job was to start in March the following year so that it would open in time for the holiday shopping season. The men were excited to hear the news, especially since they thought the hotel would be their last job for a while. They had worked jobs in the winter time before, so they knew how to prepare for it.

Between the hotel job and preparing to move, Xander was burning the candle at both ends. He was basically starting over and needed to make his new house feel like a home. Between getting the inspections done for the house and the endless paperwork, he didn't see much of Brie and was beyond elated to spend the first night in his house.

He closed the door after tipping each delivery man fifty dollars for transporting his king-size bedroom set and pillow-top mattress. He was glad for the latter because he was sick of sleeping on an air mattress. The rest of the furniture would be delivered the next day, and he was excited because Brie was on her way over with dinner. He would finally be able to show her his new place. He had planned on going to some department stores to get miscellaneous items but wanted to wait until she arrived.

When the doorbell sounded, he had just finished putting a new black-and-silver comforter set on his bed and couldn't wait to break it in with Brie. Clothed in a green tank top, blue jeans, and bare feet, he opened the door with a big grin.

"Hey, Brie."

"Hi, Xander," she greeted him wearing a purple low-cut top and white skirt. She had takeout from a Chinese restaurant and a small duffle bag. The AC was on high, and she grinned when Xander kissed her on the cheek.

"I won't tell you I got lost," she mentioned, and he shook his head slowly. "This is it, huh?" she asked, looking around the entryway and liked what she saw.

"Yes, ma'am. Let me give you the grand tour." Xander showed her around, and he liked the look of approval on her face. Of course, he still had some decorating to do, but Brie absolutely loved the house.

"This is such an amazing place. I'm glad you took your time and found something you liked," Brie told him, and they quickly ate the fried rice and egg rolls.

"Thank you. I wasn't going to rush the process. The suite I had at the hotel was nice, but I'm glad to be in my own place," Xander replied as he grabbed two cans of cola out the fridge. He had gone grocery shopping and got cleaning supplies earlier that morning, so that was one less thing he had to worry about.

"Something tells me you're going to be downstairs in your man cave a lot."

Xander chuckled. "Nah, just when the fellas come for a visit. Thanks for coming over early."

"It's not a problem. Do you know which stores you want to go to?"

Xander named off four stores, and Brie cocked her head at him. "That's a lot."

"I know, and for showing my gratitude for helping me shop, when we get back, I can give you a nice back rub."

"You're doing more than that," she said giving him a saucy look, and he gave her a hard slap across the ass as they left the house.

****

Starr was so excited Al was coming back home today. He was a traveling salesman and had been gone for several weeks. Starr ended up selling the house and moved into a penthouse in the apartment building where Casey lived. She knew it was a temporary situation because Al had promised her they would move into a bigger place once he got back.

She never pictured herself being with an overweight, white man, but if he was willing to take care of her, that was perfect. She didn't love Al by any means and didn't remain faithful to him while he traveled, but he didn't need to know that. With wine chilling, and a smile on her face, she was ready to talk to him about their wedding plans.

If he started talking about not wanting to be married right now, she knew exactly how to change his mind. She found that every time she gave Al some head, he agreed with her on any and everything. Her only objective in life was to be a pampered wife, and she'd do whatever it took to make it happen. She had already had a big, fancy wedding with Xander, so she had no qualms about doing things in Vegas this time. She was wearing a gold, silk robe and ran toward the door when she heard Al open it. Starr stopped in her tracks when she saw how old and disheveled he looked in his wrinkled and stained brown suit. He had bags under his eyes, and he hadn't shaved. He clearly wasn't the handsome, suave man she had met a few weeks ago.

"Hi, honey. I ordered dinner, and it should be here in a few minutes. Why don't you go take a shower, and I'll make you a drink," Starr suggested as she touched the lapel of his jacket, mentally rolling her eyes. She didn't like catering to him, but she knew that would be over once she got a ring and her hands on his bank account.

"I'm not staying. I came to return this." He informed her as he held up the penthouse key and placed it on the hall table.

"What? Why are you returning the key?"

"I'm going back home. This was fun at the beginning, but now it's too much. I think you're expecting me to give you more than I'm ready for. I like being a bachelor where I can come and go as I please," Al stated to Starr in a lazy tone.

Her heart was hammering at his words, not believing them. "Al, you said we'd get married. You promised to take care of me!"

"Yeah, I did. But I thought you would get a shitload of money from your divorce. I didn't think you was going to sign the papers without getting a dime from your ex." He had planned on going on a spending spree with Starr's money, but since there was no cash, there was no reason to keep pretending.

"Al, please! You have money, that's what you told me. You said you would take care of me, and I believed you."

"I'm sorry, Starr," he shrugged before opening the door. "Don't lose my number, though. You're a good lay." Starr slid down to the floor as she watched Al walk out. She couldn't believe it. Everything she had done had been based on Al's promises, and now, she was worried about her future.

The money she had gotten from the house would only last so long, especially since the rent for the penthouse was two thousand a month. Not to mention the money she spent to support her drug addiction. Thinking about that caused Starr to get up and run to the bathroom.

There was already a thin line of coke ready to be snorted from her earlier usage. Bending down, she snorted the drug and settled on the floor near the tub. She closed her eyes with a serene smile and dug inside her robe to finger herself. She was in this position because Xander had left her. *He's probably shacked up with that hotel bitch! Brie brainwashed Xander into divorcing me, and I'm going to fix that,* Starr said to herself as she came to a climax. She'd go talk to Xander, profess their love for one another, and they would be back together... one way or another.

****

A few days later, Brie had met Xander at his office so they could go out for lunch. It was a slow, rainy Wednesday afternoon, and it was perfect weather for snuggling under a blanket.

"Where do you want to go for lunch?" Xander asked her as they were sitting side by side on the couch.

"I'm thinking soul food. Some black-eyed peas and fried okra would be great right now." Xander smiled when Brie did a dance when she said it.

"You're so happy about it. That sounds good to me."

Brie had decided to tell Xander that she loved him today. She wasn't expecting for him to say it back, but it was on her heart to not let another day go by and he not know.

"Have you talked to your dad recently?"

"About a week ago. They had just left New Zealand."

"That is truly a grand cruise Theo is on," he commented, and Brie nodded.

"I know. I just wonder what he's going to do when he gets back home."

"He could do a lot. Make some repairs around the house, write a song, adopt some birds."

Brie laughed until she had tears in her eyes, and she leaned on him until the laughter subsided. "What is he going to do with birds? You are nuts."

"Speaking of nuts…"

Brie's eyebrows went up, and she folded her arms. "What about them? I believe they were well tended to three days ago." She reminded him, and he smiled that sexy grin that she loved.

"Oh, they were, believe that. But we've been talking, and we agree that you should come over to my house tonight."

"Is that right?" Xander nodded and took her hand in his. "I have some questions about you having a conversation with your nuts, but I'll think about it and give you my answer after lunch."

"Come on, baby. I love you. Don't keep me in suspense." Brie's mind warped at what had just come out of Xander's mouth. Her palms felt clammy, and it felt like her heart skipped a beat. She was certain that it had slipped out, and he wasn't aware that he had said it. Brie had to admit that she unquestionably loved how it sounded when he said it to her. It came out with pure confidence, and she hoped he really meant it.

"Xander, do you know what—" Brie stopped speaking when the office door opened, and Starr snuck in. Her hair was standing all over her head, the jeans and shirt she had on were wrinkled, and her nose was red and bulbous.

"Starr, what are you doing here?" Xander was shocked to see the way she looked. She never used to leave the house looking less than pristine, and he knew she was on something because she kept sniffing and was fidgety.

"Oh my God! You look so good, Xander. How have you

been?"

"I've been fine. What are you doing here?" he repeated his question as Brie stood up and walked over to the desk; Starr giving her an evil look.

"I need to talk to you. Let's go out to lunch, and we can speak in private," Starr said, rubbing her nose and approaching him at the same time.

"I already have plans, and we don't have anything to talk about."

"Please, Xander. I miss you so much, darling. We need to get back together," she pleaded with him, grabbing onto his shirt sleeve.

"Starr, that's not going to happen. I'm sorry, but you need to leave," Xander said firmly, and she knew he meant it. Starr looked in his eyes and wished she hadn't seen the look of disconnect and detachment. Big tears fell from her eyes as she reached inside her purse, pulled out a .38 special gun and aimed it at Brie.

Brie let out a loud gasp and threw her hands up as she backed away. Xander's heart began to throb erratically when he saw the gun shaking in her hands. He knew Starr wasn't in a stable state of mind and had to talk her down before she hurt someone.

"Hey, Starr, you don't need that. We can talk right now," Xander said in a cajoling tone as he began to inch toward the gun's line of vision between it and Brie.

"Don't move!" she screamed, wiping at her face and smearing snot on her cheek.

"OK, Starr. I won't." He was hoping someone in the hall would hear the raised voices and call either the police or security.

"She's the reason we're not together. I have to get rid of her so we can be happy again," Starr said the last part so softly, he almost felt sorry for her.

"Starr, Brie isn't the reason we're not together anymore."

"But we could be. We can get married again. I'll be so loving and faithful to you this time. We can have a baby and everything."

Brie silently thanked Xander for trying to talk some sense into Starr. She evidently had reached a crazy point of no return, and she hoped he could get the gun away from her. She tried to stay calm at the situation. She had never had a gun pointed at her before, and she didn't like how wide and glassy Starr's eyes were. By the looks of things, she had been on a downward spiral since the divorce.

"We can't do that, not right now."

"You're right, honey. You're so smart, Xander. We can go on another honeymoon and then we can have a baby," Starr acknowledged in a high-pitched laugh, and the gun discharged with a loud pop that bounced off the walls of the room. The impact caused Brie to get thrown back against the wall, and she slumped down to the floor in an unconscious heap.

"Brie!" Xander ran over to her and scrambled next to her on the ground. He flipped her over and saw that she had been shot in her shoulder, close to the neck area and a lot of blood was emitting from the wound. He took off his jacket and pressed it to the hole, pushing her hair off her face. Starr dropped the weapon and covered her mouth, surprised she had fired the gun.

She went over to Xander and began to pull on his arm. Marshall came in to investigate the noise he heard, not expecting any of what he saw, especially Starr.

"Call an ambulance!" Xander shouted to him, and

Marshall pulled out his cell phone as he went to ensure the safety of the employees.

"Xander, c'mon! We have to go!" Starr's voice trembled, and he shrugged her off before cradling Brie's pale face with blood stained hands.

"Stay with me, Brie. You just hold on, dammit!"

Starr noticed Xander wasn't paying her any mind, and she went back to her purse, where she pulled out a vial of drugs. The paramedics wheeled Brie out the building as the police were rushing in to apprehend Starr. He didn't care what they did with her or if she ended up in jail. All he knew was that Brie had lost a lot of blood, and he was more than worried as the ambulance sped toward the hospital.

****

Four hours later, Xander was sitting next to Brie's hospital bed. When they had arrived at Northwestern Hospital, she had been rushed to surgery to retrieve the bullet. She ended up needing a transfusion due to the blood loss. The doctor had told Xander that the bullet had entered the supraspinatus area just under the left clavicle bone, and had it landed a few more inches to the right, the outcome would've been worse. Aside from having to wear a sling, Brie would survive, and that's all Xander cared about.

The police had arrived while Brie was in surgery, and Xander gave them a statement. Starr ended up being arrested for carrying an unregistered gun, drug possession, and assault with intent to kill. Marshall, Natalie, and Qyle had come and gone, but Xander refused to leave. The latter had informed him that she would try to get in contact with Theo to let him know what had happened.

Brie had been moved to a private room, and the doctor said that he could stay until visiting hours were over with. Xander felt fully responsible for what went down. He didn't think Starr would do anything that extreme. If he had seen any inkling of mental instability in the years they were together, he would've done something about it a long time ago. In addition to going to jail, he hoped Starr would get the help she needed.

Xander had dozed off while waiting for Brie to wake up, and when he sluggishly opened his eyes, he saw she was up and looking at him. "Hey. How are you feeling?" He stood up and leaned over the bed.

299

"Like I have a hole in my body," she replied in a raspy voice. She winced when she tried moving her arm and glanced up at him.

"Are you OK, Xander? You didn't get hurt, did you?"

"No, I'm fine, baby. I'm so sorry, Brie. I—"

She pressed her fingers to his lips, and their eyes were glued to each other. "Xander, don't you apologize. You tried to stop it from getting worse."

"A lot of good it did. You got shot, Brie." Xander let out a deep breath and lowered his head. Brie cupped his neck with her uninjured arm, feeling his pulse beating at a rapid pace. He pressed his lips to her forehead, and she moved toward his embrace.

"I love you, Brie. I thought I lost you today." Xander felt tears fall on his arm, and he looked at her. He was taken aback when he saw a cheerful smile.

"I know. I heard you say it in your office."

"Yes, I did say it. I was wondering if you had heard me."

"I did. I love you too. So very much." Xander closed his eyes at her declaration and leaned forward to give her a hard, emotional kiss.

"I was going to tell you today." Brie disclosed, and he kissed her forehead.

"Looks like I beat you to it."

"It's not a competition, Xander."

"I know, but just be prepared to hear it from me every day."

"Not if I beat you to it," she voiced just before he closed the distance between them and kissed her again.

Epilogue

Two years later…

Xander stomped the snow off his boots on the rug in the garage before he walked into the warm house. It had been hell driving from Midway Airport to New Lenox, and he was glad he didn't run into any holiday traveling issues. Christmas was three weeks away, and it snowed a few more inches the two days he had been away. Luggage in hand, he trotted up the stairs and headed in the direction of the main bedroom. Lola had texted him that they and Theo had left around four that afternoon, but he knew that didn't stop her from calling in to check on Brie every half hour.

She was probably driving Brie crazy, but he knew she didn't mind. Walking into the bedroom, Xander looked around and saw Brie sleeping on a chaise lounge and let out a deep, calming breath. He took a fast shower to get the airport smell off him and walked toward her as he put on a clean pair of sweatpants and a T-shirt. He sat down next to his wife and admired her body. At nine months pregnant, Brie was beautiful and glowing like never before. She had gained most of her pregnant weight in her tummy, which was to be expected when one was having twins. They had found out in her second trimester that they were having a boy and a girl and felt doubly blessed.

He could tell she had taken a bath not too long ago. She smelled of the rose oil she used to keep away stretch marks, but a few had popped up. Her robe was open to expose her naked body, and he started to rub his hand across her round stomach.

"Hey, guys. Daddy's home." Xander felt a series of kicks and movements and he grinned widely. "Calm down. You're going to wake your mama."

"It's too late for that." He lifted his head and saw Brie smiling at him.

"Hey, beautiful."

"Hiya, sexy. When did you get home?" He leaned forward and gave her a slow open mouth smooch.

"A few minutes ago," he answered after the kiss ended.

"How was the trip? What did they say?" He let out a low laugh and sat next to her legs, and she propped up on her elbows.

"Well, the first-class flight to New York was great. I met

with the VP of special planning for a few hours. I asked some questions, he asked some questions. Long story short, I signed a contract to be a guest commentator for the Super Bowl," he replied, and Brie squealed as she hugged him.

"That's great! Congratulations, honey."

"Thanks. They'll fly me out a few days before the game. There will be a meet and greet event with other pro players. We'll get to take some pictures and sign some autographs."

"You know you're going to love it," Brie remarked, and he smiled. Xander told her how much he would get paid and her eyes got big.

"Holy crap! That's a ton of cash."

"That's the kids college tuition."

Brie was glad that Xander would have the chance to be around football again. She knew he missed it and would love the feel of being in that environment once more. Things were continuously looking up for them, and she thanked their favor each day. The hotel renovations quadrupled the guest accommodations, and after Faith's spy movie came out and was a box-office success, it had added to the grandeur of the hotel. With the spike in reservations and visitors, Brie had to hire more staff members.

Business was good, and Theo had stepped back into his former shoes while Brie was on maternity leave. Starr had been sentenced to five years in jail, and in her last letter to Xander, she had told him she had been diagnosed with HIV. He wasn't surprised by the news, given the fact that she had unprotected sex with several guys. He threw the letter away without responding to it. Starr had to live with the consequence of her actions and refused to think about the past when Brie was his future.

A year after the shooting, Xander and Brie had gotten married on a private beach in Hawaii with their parents and friends in attendance. He felt that Brie should've had a big wedding, but she asserted that she wanted a small one and loved the idea of it. S&T was doing well and steadily growing. After working the last two winters, the crew was happy to have this one off, so they could spend time with their families and travel.

"I really missed you," Brie said in a throaty voice that got his blood roasting.

"Is that right?" he asked as the hand that was caressing her belly had moved down her body. She nodded and bit her bottom lip in pleasure when he inserted two fingers inside her and found Brie already moist. Xander had to admit that sex with his pregnant wife was off the chain. She was one of those rare women whose pregnancy caused her sex drive to increase, and he didn't complain about it. Brie was on him two to three times a day, and he had to make sure it was safe while she was expecting.

The doctor had told them to go for it and that it would make the delivery easier. Xander had to calm her down in the last trimester, but they kept at it. Brie wrapped her right arm around his neck to pull him closer for a kiss as his free hand massaged her breasts. They were extra sensitive and full of milk, and she went up two bra sizes. They kissed each other slowly as his knees went between her legs to open them.

Brie's hand traveled down his shirt and dug inside his sweat pants to cup his erect penis. "Please, honey," she begged in a gentle tone.

He stood up and pulled his shirt off as she tugged his pants down to greedily take the bulging head into her attentive mouth. He let her go at it for a few minutes because she was so good at giving head. Moaning deeply, his hands curled into tight fists when he felt her tongue swirling over his length and cheeks tightening around him. Xander stepped forward and bent one leg on the furniture to position himself over her.

Brie had turned on her left side, and he lifted her leg to rest on top of his thigh. She licked her lips when she felt Xander inch inside her and start a passionate back-and-forth motion. He braced one hand on top of the furniture to use as leverage while the other hand cupped and fiddled with her huge breast.

"Are you OK, baby?" he asked, in a panting voice while still moving inside of her.

"Yes." She hissed, wailing when he pinched her nipples. Xander wanted to pound into her harder, but the slow mating was good for right now. He couldn't wait for them to restart their usual sexual practices again after she was cleared by the physician. Brie's feminine sounds were driving him mad, and he saw the ecstasy on her face. Brie turned her head to look at him, and he bent down to take her lips. Xander knew she had two orgasms already and gripped the edge in a strong hold as he had a spine-tingling release while feeling her milk him.

He got behind her as they both took the time to catch their

breaths; his right hand stroking her belly. "That's the good stuff, honey," she admitted, and he smiled.

"Sometimes I think you only like me for my body," Xander retorted, and she kissed his hand.

"First of all, I love you. Second, you have a kick ass body, and third, I can't help it if you're a sexy man beast who gives your wife immense pleasure."

He looked up, contemplating her words. "You do make a good point. Let's go eat."

He got dressed, and she threw on a long shirt with Christmas decorations on it and matching socks. He helped Brie downstairs to the kitchen where he turned on the pot of beef stew that Theo had made before he left. Brie cut up the buttery cornbread into squares while Xander went to turn on the holiday lights.

He saw piles of presents under the Christmas tree and knew the pending grandparents had gone crazy in his absence with gifts for the babies. Going back into the kitchen, he saw Brie had set the kitchen table and was carrying the cornbread to the microwave when he stopped her.

"Let me do that." She patted his arm and opened the fridge

to take out two bottles of water to go with dinner.

"What happened here while I was away?" He wondered once they had dinner in front of them, and the radio was playing festive music in the background.

"My dad and your parents stayed here for those two days because they didn't want me here by myself. We went to the Water Tower Place to shop, and they walked out with like fifty bags apiece for the twins. Our dads bought Xavier a six-hundred-piece train set, and Lola got Makayla an antique tea set. They wouldn't let me see the rest of the items they got."

Xander desired to keep the X-name tradition and wanted to name their son Xavier, which Brie had no problem with. Baby girl Makayla would take Brie's mother's name as her middle one; giving the infant the moniker Makayla Cassie Sterling.

"They have lost their minds." He concluded, shaking his head while blowing on the thick broth.

"They're just excited to be grandparents. We won't have any problems getting a babysitter if we need one." Brie revealed, and Xander nodded in agreement. While she was eating, the babies were having a field day with a lot of kicking and moving. She took his hand and placed it on the side of her tummy.

It always amazed Xander to feel his children moving and growing inside Brie. He loved every single part of her pregnancy, including the outrageous food cravings. Yes, she did send him out in a thunderstorm to get bags of sour cream and onion flavored potato chips. Brie was thankful Xander had been there to enjoy every single milestone with her. She knew she had driven him batty a few times, especially the three times she made him repaint the baby's rooms.

"Either they're having a party or they're happy you're eating beef stew."

She chuckled, eating a piece of cornbread. "I think it's both."

The dishwasher had been loaded after they finished dinner, and Brie followed Xander into the living room as they held hands. They sat on the sectional with Brie reclining against his chest between his muscular thighs. Xander's hand were on her swelling front, moving them in soothing circles. A fire was crackling in the fireplace, and with the Christmas lights, it made for a peaceful, romantic ambience. Brie was humming to a holiday song, watching the dancing decorations, and her hands were on Xander's knees.

"Are you good, babe?" she asked, due to his silence.

"Yes. Just thinking."

"About what?"

"About how perfect this moment is. How content and tranquil you make me feel. Thank you so much, Brie."

She sat up and searched his eyes with a frown on his face. "What for?"

"Hell, where do I start? For loving me, marrying me. For carrying my kids and being such a caring, tender, funny, and devoted wife to me. I'm beyond happy, and it's because of you, Brie Sterling." Xander had clasped her face at the last part and gave a soft peck.

She placed her hand over his heart, deepening the kiss as tears flowed down her face. "You're not supposed to make a pregnant woman cry," she mentioned, and he tweaked her nose. "I love you so much, Xander. I couldn't imagine being this satisfied and loved. You are my soulmate, and I am honored to be the mother of your children."

"So does that mean we can have some more?" Xander

probed and she was taken aback.

"Let's see… since I'm in the middle of cooking these two buns in the oven now. Perhaps we can table that thought for a few years," Brie replied, causing Xander to explode with laughter.

They continued talking until they fell asleep on the couch. When Xander woke up hours later, he let out a big yawn and saw that it was past four a.m. from the clock on the wall. Brie wasn't on the couch and he got up to get something to drink from the kitchen. He figured she had gone to bed and would join her after getting some water. When he turned the light on in the kitchen, he saw her leaning against the counter, and her face was masked with pain.

"Brie! What is it?" he rushed over to her. Brie's body tightened as another contraction ripped through her body. After it passed, she let out a shallow breath and leaned against Xander.

"We need to get to the hospital," she told him in a low, tense voice.

He nodded and jetted upstairs to get what she needed. He reappeared seconds later with pants for her and the bag for the babies. They donned boots and coats, and he ushered Brie to his truck in the garage. She concentrated on her breathing as Xander carefully drove them to the hospital. It had snowed overnight, and the streets hadn't been plowed yet.

"When did the pains start?" Xander inquired, squeezing her hand.

"Maybe thirty minutes ago."

"Fuck, Brie! Why didn't you wake me up?"

"I thought it was indigestion," she replied softly with her eyes closed.

"You're gonna get it when we get home." Brie let out a small smile; knowing Xander would never hurt her. He was nervous about the birth, and it showed. They got to the hospital in record time and he parked in the designated area before escorting her in. It was a flutter of activity as Brie was admitted, Xander filled out paperwork and called their parents after he was done with that task.

Luckily, Brie's doctor was already on call at the hospital, and she came into the room twenty minutes later. "Hey Brie and Xander. I wasn't expecting you guys for another few weeks," Dr. Penny Hicks said to them as she picked up Brie's chart. She was a middle-aged black woman with a small, brown Afro.

"Yeah, well, tell that to Thing 1 and Thing 2," Brie responded as she sat perched upon several pillows; her fingers interlocked with Xander's.

Dr. Hicks tittered, flipping through the file. "The nurse said you're already three centimeters dilated." She said the last part more to herself, and the married couple was quiet as Dr. Hicks checked Brie's cervix and pulled out her stethoscope. Brie had been hooked up to the fetal monitor and both heartbeats could be heard loud and clear.

"Doc, she's a few weeks early. Is that okay?" Xander questioned with a worried expression on his face.

"Yes. Brie is thirty-eight weeks, which is not too bad. I'll keep her on a monitor and both babies have a good weight with strong heartbeats. Since Brie's water hasn't broken yet, we may have to do it, but let's give it a few hours. Mrs. Sterling, I suggest you get some rest, and we'll come back to check on you later," Dr. Hicks suggested as she made notes in the chart and strolled out the room.

"Are you still mad at me?" Brie asked her husband,

turning to face him.

Xander blew out a breath and kissed her hand. "No, babe. Just... don't do that again. If you're in any type of pain, tell me." She nodded and settled back on the pillows.

"How are you feeling?"

"I'm a little sleepy."

"Get some rest, honey. I'll stay up in case Dr. Hicks comes back in."

"You aren't going to sleep?" Brie asked him, yawning,

"No, I'm too wired right now." She nodded and watched as he turned off the overhead light. Brie closed her eyes while Xander stayed true to his word and stayed up; his eyes watching the fetal monitor. Their parents arrived almost an hour later, and they spoke in hushed tones while Brie slept, and he filled them in.

Ten hours later, Brie's water had broken, and she was finally ready to start delivering her children after fully dilating. She covered her eyes as tears ran down her face. She had been pushing for a few minutes, but it felt like forever. The pain was agonizing, and all she wanted to do was go home. The birthing classes hadn't prepared her for this level of discomfort, and she was pissed about that.

"Brie, you are doing so good. Just a few more pushes," Dr. Hicks encouraged from behind her mask. Xander helped her sit up, and she pushed again as sweat dripped down her face. The grandparents-to-be were standing to the side, and they had on scrubs; Lola and Theo were ready with their cameras to take pictures of their grandchildren. Brie pushed again and soon the room was filled with cries of the first-born twin.

"Makayla is here," the doctor announced, handing the baby girl to the waiting nurse. Xander didn't look at his daughter as he kept coaching Brie through the rest of the birthing process. Seven minutes later, Xavier was born; his screams just as piercing as his sister's. Brie fell back on the pillows, beyond exhausted, and Xander gave her quick kisses on her face.

"You did good, baby. I love you, Brie." She let out a small smile as Dr. Hicks was dealing with the afterbirth.

"Go see them," she whispered, and he nodded. He walked toward them, and after they were cleaned and checked, he was handed a swaddled Makayla. She was looking at him with small eyes, and his heart turned over. He kissed her forehead and handed her to Lola; the grandparents cooing. Xavier's eyes were closed when he was placed in his father's arms, but that didn't stop him from clutching the tip of Xander's finger.

He turned so Brie could see her babies, but saw she was knocked out. Dr. Hicks allowed Xander to stay in the room with the twins while Brie slept. The Sterlings and Theo had left to get something to eat and to visit the gift shop. Xander had told them to not buy out the whole place, but he knew it fell on deaf ears. Two hours had passed, and Brie finally woke up. Everything was quiet in the room, and she grinned when she heard Xander talking to the children.

"That's how your mom and I met. She won't tell you, but she wanted me in college."

"I see I'll have to tell them the truth when they get older." Xander looked up, and he smiled sheepishly, walking her way with a baby.

"Damn, you're gorgeous. How do you feel?"

Brie blushed at his statement and sighed. "Sore and exhausted."

"I know you are." He leaned over the bed, and she slowly and carefully sat up with the help of the hospital bed. "Here is your son, Xavier."

Brie looked at the boy, and her eyes began to water. She was finally able to put a face to one of the babies she felt moving inside her for months. He was so handsome, and she couldn't believe she was finally a mother.

"He's perfect. He looks like you," she said with a light laugh.

"And here is our daughter and oldest by seven minutes, Makayla." Xander handed her the first twin and made sure she had enough pillows under both arms so they could be supported while she held them for the first time. Brie smiled at her daughter and knew she would be a beautiful little girl.

Both were sleeping, and she kissed their faces. "They are stunning, Xander," she said on a shudder as more tears fell down her cheeks.

"I know, honey." He sat next to her on the bed, and she placed her head on his shoulder. "You did good, babe." Xander let her know, brushing her tears away, and she closed her eyes to thank God for her kids, husband and family.

"There are two of them and two of us. You think we can handle this?" Brie asked him, kissing the underside of

Xander's jaw.

"We got this, Brie. We're a team, and these two little ones are going to be so loved. Besides, we have three willing and able grandparents we can call in as backup for when they give us hell."

Brie laughed at that, her eyes never leaving the sleeping, innocent duo. "I like that plan, but like you said, my love, we got this."

The End

Be sure to LIKE our Major Key Publishing page on Facebook!

Made in the USA
Middletown, DE
04 May 2019